DEAD LOCK

SIMON FOX

nosy crow

First published in the UK in 2023 by Nosy Crow Ltd
Wheat Wharf, 27a Shad Thames,
London, SE1 2XZ, UK

Nosy Crow Eireann Ltd
44 Orchard Grove, Kenmare,
Co Kerry, V93 FY22, Ireland

Nosy Crow and associated logos are trademarks and/or registered
trademarks of Nosy Crow Ltd

ISBN: 978 1 83994 442 0

A CIP catalogue record for this book will be available from
the British Library.

Printed and bound in Great Britain by Clays Ltd, Elcograf S.p.A.
Typeset by Tiger Media

Papers used by Nosy Crow are made from wood grown in
sustainable forests.

1 3 5 7 9 10 8 6 4 2

www.nosycrow.com

For Joe Wicks, Tony Blackburn and Kevin Feige. For keeping me going when times were tough.

– S.F

MONDAY
9.24 p.m.

Monday night is race night.

No delays, no postponements, no excuses. Just me and him and who can open whatever's on the table first. Boy against man. And I hate losing.

It had started when I was just messing around with Dad's police-issue handcuffs. It had been stupid really, but I was bored and I'd wanted to see if I could close them and still squeeze my hand out. I'd kind of folded my palm over into my fingers and pulled hard to get free. It had hurt a bit, but I didn't care. Then I'd clicked them a tiny bit tighter and tried again. Then a tiny bit more...

And then I was stuck.

Dad had half looked up from the TV. "You need the key," he said.

I didn't want to give in, but I was going to rip my hand off if I didn't. "Where is it?" I asked.

He looked at me then sighed. "I lost it ages ago," he

said. He was staring at me like he didn't know how I was going to react but I was just confused.

"You must have it," I said. "Don't you need it?"

And then he kind of looked proud of himself and didn't say anything, but I could see the slight smile on the corner of his lips and I wanted to know why.

"What?" I said. "I'm stuck. You need to get me out."

But Dad just shook his head. He got up slowly and walked over to the table where I was sitting. Part of me was thinking that he was checking to see if I'd done any homework, and I didn't want to get into a row, but the other part of me wanted to get the stupid cuff off my wrist so I sat still while he leaned across and flicked over a few pages of the science textbook that I hadn't even looked at. Then he picked up the other end of the cuffs.

"Stuck with homework or stuck with these?"

"Both," I said. "Now, are you going to let me out or what?"

I could feel the frustration starting to grow in my chest because he was taking too long, and I thought about the exercises the counsellor had given me but why the hell should I do them when he still had that half-smile on his face and was nodding his head like some old wise monk or something.

"I wonder if this is the solution," he said, and leaned forward, slamming the open cuff on to the leg of the table where it meets the top. I was stuck there and he was laughing, which was crazy because I couldn't remember the last time he'd laughed.

I tried to grab his arm, but he swerved out of the way and my hand jerked hard against the cuffs, which made him laugh even more. Then I was laughing too, even though I wanted to be angry.

Dad had this big grin on his face and he told me that when I finished my homework he would let me out.

I told him to stop being annoying and he told me to tell my face to stop being annoying, which was possibly the most annoying thing he could have said but all I could do was kind of laugh and moan and shout out in frustration.

"Come on, Dad. Give me the key!"

There was a pause and he looked at me like he was wondering whether to stop because the laughter had been good and if he carried on it could all go wrong.

"I told you. I lost it," he said.

"So how will you get me out when I've done my homework?"

He looked around him. The table was pushed back, trapping the two chairs we didn't use against the old sideboard. It was covered in stuff he hadn't got around to sorting, even though it had been ages now, and he moved some of it around before he pulled out a pile of papers held together with a large paperclip.

"With this," he said, and he took the paperclip off the papers and held it up for me to see.

I stared at it then I looked at the lock on the cuffs. "How?" I said.

He smiled. "Do your homework and I'll show you."

But that didn't feel fair and now he'd gone too far and something must've flashed in my eyes because he knew it too. Because I'd been sitting there for ages and I didn't want to do my stupid homework and I could feel the fire in my mind and the pressure in my shoulders and I wondered if I pulled and kicked and stamped and ripped I could just smash this stupid table to pieces. I wanted to swear at him and break and tear my wrist from my arm then scream until the whole world stopped, because he shouldn't be doing this, should he? He should be making things easy so I

4

could slide through the day and go to bed then slide through the next one until at some point the future would happen and everything would be fine again.

Except there was a tear in his eye and suddenly I thought, *Please don't cry in front of me*, because hearing it was bad but seeing it was more than I could handle and he was just holding that paperclip like it had all the answers.

He reached out with it and then put it on the table, holding my eyes with his for a long time. He kind of smiled at me and maybe I smiled back, I don't know, but he went and sat back down and I picked it up.

And that's how it all started.

Because I didn't give up. It took me an hour but I didn't give up. My wrist hurt, my fingers were sore and I definitely didn't do any more homework, but I didn't give up. And I got the cuffs off.

Dad had gone to sleep on the sofa again. He knew watching me would just wreck it, so he ignored me and watched the telly until he nodded off, and in a strange way I got this mad buzz from opening them without him seeing. I was about to wake him up, but then I had a better idea.

I tidied up as quietly as I could, packing up my books,

clearing away the dinner things into the dishwasher and straightening things for tomorrow. Then I went back into the living room and turned off the TV.

Dad jerked as he woke up. There was panic in his eyes and it shot through me but then he saw where he was and calmed down. It took him a moment to remember what had been happening but then he looked at me and smiled.

"You got them off then?" he said.

I nodded and smiled back as I put the paperclip down on top of the TV, just out of his reach, then pointed at the cuffs that now fixed his wrist firmly to the radiator behind him.

"Your turn," I said.

Then I turned off the light and went up to bed.

The next week he said, "I thought you might want to see this."

It was just a dumb padlock, but it was one that one of his crooks had tried to open but couldn't. He showed me what to do and we both tried and then I could open that too. Then when we had our counselling, Theresa didn't look quite so timid and said whatever we were doing was doing good, so keep it up.

"Really?" he asked, and I listened outside the door so I could hear her response.

"Yes, really," she said.

So we did.

Monday night became race night.

Homework waits; I don't cook and I'm just buzzing. I set up the table before he gets home, with the old brown cloth, the pot of grease and the timer. And my set of tools.

"Because that's fair," I say. "You get to choose the lock; I should choose the tools."

He shrugs and grins and laughs and says OK, so the pale-blue leather case of seventy-year-old dentist tools I found at a car boot sale sits on the table between us. But I'm still not sure they'll be enough, because who knows what he's brought for us to open.

He holds out his hands and says I should trust him not to cheat, but it's all about cheating, isn't it, and he's got that smile on his face. I say I've got to have something on my side, so he says how about we both choose one thing that's modern to go with it and I can choose first. *Fine*, I think. *We'll do that.* Except the first night it's a couple of simple three-coil padlocks. Should be easy, right, so I grin at him and

7

take the two-millimetre wire and put it on my side of the table. He grins back and picks up the head torch.

Then he turns off the light.

Dad brings home all sorts of stuff. I don't know where he gets most of it. From work or a junk shop or maybe from one of the engineers the prevention team uses. Then we race. I used to get the feeling he was letting me win but when I surprise him by springing open an early Victorian Webley in less than a minute, he looks at me with a strange expression like pride and shock at the same time.

"You really are an alien," he says. "Almost six feet at thirteen and breaking safes in fifty-five seconds. I thought your mum loved *Star Wars* a bit too much." He stares at me for a long time before slapping his hands suddenly on his knees and getting up to grab another beer from the fridge. "Go on then," he says. "Do it again, only slower this time so I can see."

The very best race nights are the ones where we try and try and try, but we just can't get the thing open. That's when the time flies, and I find myself leaning over the table holding the torch, trying to angle the magnets while Dad eases the mechanism, slowly and silently, patient like you can't believe, both of us holding our breath, waiting for the tiny whisper of magic.

Click.

The lock is open so it's time to tidy up because it's school tomorrow and he has to iron his shirt for work and he'll probably be gone when I get up and make sure I get some washing powder when I shop and hurry, hurry, hurry because the race is done and it's way past time for bed.

But those are the nights when I can't sleep and I know it's the same for him.

I sit at the top of the stairs like I used to; when they would laugh or argue or make plans or talk about me. When I would stare at that photo of them on the wall and listen to the tick of the clock, leaning on the banister and trying not to fall asleep. Except now the clock doesn't tick and the only sound is Dad padding around until eventually I hear the click of the light switch and the slight creak of the living-room door. Then I hold my breath and creep back to my room, slipping into bed just in time to see the handle turn and Dad's face appear at the door.

"Good one tonight," he says.

"Yeah," I say. "I didn't think we were going to do it."

Dad leans against the door frame. He is still in the darkness, outlined in the light from the landing.

"We can always do it," he says, "if we keep trying. We've just got to keep changing the angles and find a way. If one of us can't do it, the other one will."

He straightens up then reaches for the door handle. "You sleeping all right these days?"

I nod, although I don't know if he can see. "Better," I say, and he smiles.

"Me too," he says. "Goodnight, Archie. Love you."

He closes the door and I lie there in the darkness, thinking of cogs, wheels and the magic sound of locks opening. I think about Mum and I think about Dad and I try to remember what it was like before we had race night but it is hard, so then I try to guess what we're going to have next time and then I think about what I am going to practise and I wonder if Dad is planning too.

But then this week's race night comes and Dad doesn't come home. He doesn't call and he doesn't even send a message. And I have a horrible feeling that something is terribly wrong.

MONDAY
11.58 p.m.

The phone buzzes once and wakes me. I roll over and look at the screen.

Esme calling.

I pick it up. "Yeah?"

"It's me."

Dad says it fast. "It's me." It used to be a joke, because it sounds like *Esme* when he says it, but there is something wrong and Dad's voice is tense, low, urgent. Now it doesn't seem so funny.

"What's up?"

"You need to get out of the house. It's not safe. Get some things and go out the back. I've got the car in Percy Road."

"Why aren't you here? Is this a part of the race?"

"No, Archie." I hear him hesitate. "Really, no," he says. "There isn't time to explain now. People are watching the house. We need to get to the station. Bring a few things but go fast. Leave your phone because they can track it. And one more thing."

I am sitting up, with my knees pulled up in front of me and my phone clamped to my right ear.

"What?"

"In my room, in my bedside table, I need you to take out the second drawer. The back of the drawer is hollow. Inside it there's an envelope and a set of keys. Bring them and come as fast as you can."

The phone goes dead and I stare at the screen for a moment, trying to work out what's going on. I run my hands through my hair then reach across to turn on the bedside light.

Then I stop myself.

Was Dad being serious? It seems like a strange sort of joke but there had been something in his voice...

Police officers get targeted sometimes, don't they?

I roll out of bed, fast, fighting to recall what he'd said, glancing at the open window then sliding on to the floor to pull on last night's clothes. I grab my black Adidas rucksack from where I've dumped it, tip all my school stuff out and shove some clean clothes into it. Then I pull on my trainers and push my wallet into my pocket.

I crawl on to the landing. Dad's room is at the front

and his curtains are open so I stay on my belly and scramble around to the bedside table. I pull at the drawer but it doesn't open. I pull again, but it seems stuck or locked or something and suddenly panic seems to wash through me. Why are people watching us? What do they want? I can almost feel the eyes through that window and I need to open this drawer so I shove my foot against the base of the unit and rip the handle back. The wood splits and the drawer comes out as a loud crack echoes around the house. My breath catches in my throat and I freeze, lying motionless in the dark, counting to ten, listening to my heartbeat in the silence.

Until, from somewhere outside, I hear the thump of a car door.

I move faster, feeling across the back of the drawer, finding the panel and sliding the wood across until I can pull out the folded envelope and the keys. I shove them in my pocket then creep out, down the stairs and into the kitchen. I put my hand on the door handle then stop.

Through the glass pane in the door, a movement catches my eye. Somewhere in the darkness there is a change in the shadows and a noise as quiet as a breath. Every muscle in my body wants to open the door and burst out but I don't. Slowly and steadily I pull my hand away from the handle. I take a step backwards, then another. Then I race back up the stairs.

The bathroom is at the side of the house, with the window open because the nights have been so hot. Through the window I can see the fence that separates our house from our neighbour's and, a little further away, the darkness of next door's garden. I crane my neck and lean out, moving a centimetre at a time, staring at the side of our house, until I am fully out, but I can't see around the wall into our back garden.

And if I can't see them, they can't see me.

I pick up my bag and sling it over my shoulder, then I stop. For seconds I feel myself almost paralysed in indecision. My fingers grip the window frame. One foot is on the sill. My muscles tense to pull me up, but my mind won't release them. Then I decide.

I dash out of the bathroom again, sliding my hand across the wall at the top of the stairs, pulling the photo off its hook as I go past, stripping the picture out of its frame, then leaving the frame on the living-room table as I grab my blue leather case of dentist tools and shove them in the pocket of my hoodie.

Now I need to get out. I race back up and lever myself out of the window. Wrapping my hands around the large black pipe that runs down from the bathroom to the ground, I slip down about three metres, then swing out my feet so they rest on the thin wooden fence between the houses. I push myself away from the wall, balancing for a moment entirely on the soles of my feet, standing tall on the fence, until I bend my knees, grab the top of the fence with my hands, and drop into next door's garden.

At the bottom of the garden there is a stone wall and behind that the garden of one of the houses in Percy Road. I sling myself over the wall then run down the side of the house, panting as I burst out into the street.

Then a hand grabs my collar.

TUESDAY
12.01 a.m.

I flinch and pull away but the figure won't let go. An arm wraps around me, dragging me so close I can feel their body heat. The other hand rises to cover my mouth.

"Don't speak, just follow," whispers Dad.

I don't have time to argue. Dad pulls me along, thirty metres down the road to where our old Volvo is parked carelessly in the street, with the big dent on my side and the engine still running.

We get in and within seconds we are moving.

"Did you bring the keys?"

"Yeah. What's going on?"

He doesn't answer but lowers his window and throws his phone out of it, hard, so it shatters on the road with a crack. I stare at him, my mind racing. I can see the whites of his knuckles and there is a tear in the sleeve of his black jumper and blood down his wrist, which has poured on to an old sweet tin on his lap. He sees me looking then picks up the tin and shoves it at me.

"Hold that," he says. "I'll explain soon. But now I need to concentrate."

His expression seems so lost it rips through me and I hold his gaze, trying to work out what it is that looks so out of control. Is it shock, maybe, or fear?

There isn't time to see. He looks back to the road then turns left, hammering the accelerator. "I'm going to go past the house," he said. "But quickly. Get in the back and tell me what you see."

I don't argue, just scramble across to the back seat and stare out of the window.

"Who am I looking for?" I ask, trying to keep the panic out of my voice. "Who are we running from?"

Dad doesn't seem to hear me. He is driving fast and muttering under his breath. "Taylor was right," he says. "They reel you in and then they've got you." And suddenly he smashes his hands down hard upon the steering wheel. "How could I be so stupid?"

I need to know what's going on. I start to ask again, "Who are we..." But before I finish we are passing our house.

I twist myself to see as we race past, and suddenly

17

my stomach feels like it's full of glass. "There's a black BMW," I say, "bumped up on to the pavement next to our drive. Two people are at the front door. There was someone in the garden earlier. I think they're trying to get in…"

We are going too fast for me to see clearly, then Dad turns left faster than I am expecting and the scene has gone.

"They were going into our house," I say, but I can feel my shoulders relaxing. Relief flows through me and I breathe out for what seems like the first time in hours. "It's all right." I put my hand on Dad's shoulder and squeeze it. "One of them had a uniform on. They were police. You can stop and go back."

I lean back in the seat and feel my hands unclench, waiting for Dad to say something, but there is just silence.

I lean forward again. "Did you hear what I said? It was police."

I am searching for his eyes in the rear-view mirror but when he looks up he shakes his head quickly.

"Not now, Archie," he says. "We need to get to the station and on a train. I'll tell you everything but it's complicated and right now you need to let me drive."

18

We are going to the train station, not the police station? For a moment I half hope I have misunderstood but I know I haven't. We fly past the turn-off to the police station and Dad ignores it. Silence falls on the car like a weight.

I climb back into the front, moving the stuff on the seat to sit down. As I pick up the tin Dad seems to wake up and shoots out his hand protectively towards it before he realises it is safe. He flicks a glance at me then stares back at the road.

"I almost found them," he says. "I almost found them, but they were expecting me."

Another car pulls out in front of us and Dad swerves hard around it, before speeding on again.

"Who?" I ask, but he ignores me.

"We've got to get out of here so I can work out what to do," he says. "I just need a few days." His eyes flick back to the tin. "But if they get that, it's all over."

We race under a railway bridge and pass another sign to the station.

"Put the tin in my bag," Dad orders, "and zip it up."

There's a plain black bag with a leather strap on the back seat. I shove the tin into it and pass it to Dad, who pulls it on to his lap. We are at the train station now, waiting at a light before going into the drop-off zone.

He turns to me. "Have you got any money?"

I've just got a fiver and a few coins in my pocket. "Not much," I say.

Dad pulls his wallet out and throws it to me. Inside it I can see the warrant card with Dad's photo and *Detective Inspector Graham Blake* written above the crest. I take a twenty-pound note then pass the wallet back and Dad jams it in his pocket again. Then he turns to me.

"We're going to Brighton," he says. "We'll stay apart so we're harder to spot. Get a ticket but use a machine and don't draw attention to yourself. We'll get on the next train from platform three and we can talk then. But if you see me before we're on the train, you don't know me."

The lights change to amber, but he waits for another moment. I reach for the door handle, but he stretches out his hand and places it on mine. Our eyes meet and the haunted look is back on Dad's face.

"I love you, Archie," he says. "It's just for a few days until I work things out. I have to get this tin somewhere safe and I can't trust anyone, not even the police." He hesitates before continuing. "If I get some time to think, everything will be OK, I promise. Now, go."

He leans across and pushes open my door. I duck out, pulling up my hood and slinging my bag over my shoulder. The car behind revs its engine but I ignore it and move quickly towards the entrance to the station, which is still busy. As I get there, I turn to look for the car but it has moved out of sight into the drop-off point. There is nothing else to do except keep my head down and stay as close to the shadows as I can.

There are people milling around everywhere at the station and I weave through them. Businessmen in suits wait for the last train home with loosened collars and bloodshot eyes. Foreign students chatter away in some language I don't recognise, and people in ones and twos stand around tapping on their phones and talking quietly. I buy a ticket and move down the platform, trying to think back to all the times Dad would go on about his job, telling me a million little details he thought I might be interested in, even though I never really was. I'm sure he said something about surveillance but it is hard to remember so I just try to spot the cameras, then stop outside the waiting room in as close to a blind spot as I can find.

The foreign students arrive on the platform, chattering loudly, but all I can hear is the blood rushing around my head. I hunch my shoulders and stand close to them, as if I'm with them, my arms crossed and a bored look on my face. I stare straight ahead to the platform opposite and count the seconds down in my head.

And then Dad is there. He has a ticket in one hand and his black bag in the other. The urge to stop him is almost overwhelming but I resist and ignore him. He walks past, towards the other end of the platform, and then waits under the large station clock, just as the train appears in the distance.

An announcement rings out.

The next train on platform three is the twelve twenty-seven to Brighton, calling at Gatwick Airport, Haywards Heath and Brighton only.

I glance to my right and see Dad shuffle forward with everyone else. Then I stare forward as the train slows and stops in front of me.

Except the doors don't open. And a man's voice booms out across the platform.

"Police. Stay where you are. Graham Blake, do not

get on that train."

I spin round and everyone else is turning too. Two men are running along the platform towards Dad, who is ignoring them. The man in front is shouting that they are police and telling everyone to stay still. A third, uniformed, officer joins them. Then the second officer grabs the first man's shoulder and points straight at Dad, who starts to run.

But there is nowhere to go.

TUESDAY
12.28 a.m.

Two more policemen are moving down the platform from the other end and Dad almost crashes into them. They grab him and he struggles against their grip, but now all five have reached him and he has no chance. They all tumble to the floor and then they overwhelm him and drag him to his feet.

They pull his hands behind his back and he drops the bag, which falls a few paces away from them. They get handcuffs on him and he cries out in pain as they twist his arm. I can feel the adrenalin flooding through me and I start moving towards him, wanting to fight for him, to make them let him go. He is wrestling against their grip but it is pointless. All he is doing is wasting energy.

Except perhaps it is more than that. Little by little he is moving away from the bag; shuffling, twisting and finding a little more distance with every move, still thinking about keeping the tin away from the

24

police. I stare around frantically, trying to think of a way to help.

Two men, about eighteen or nineteen, are standing behind me, drinking beer from cans and watching what is going on. As the policemen twist Dad's arms behind his back, the one with orange hair sucks in his breath dramatically then laughs.

"Bet they beat him up," he says, before taking a swig and burping.

The other one shakes his head. "Too many people around," he says. "They'll give him a kicking at the station."

I spin round, shocked at what they are saying, and find myself staring at a guy with vacant brown eyes and a Chinese tattoo on his neck.

"Yeah?" the man says. "You want something?"

I can hear the police speaking to Dad as they hold him still. They are arresting him on suspicion of theft, reading him his rights, and I can feel the desperation build inside me. The other passengers are all standing and watching because the police won't let the train doors open. Another train heading towards London pulls into platform two behind us, but no one moves. And now the anger wants to burst out but I know I need to control it.

I stare at the man. "I want you to shut your face," I say, and I try to sound as tough as I can, but the guy with the orange hair just thinks it's funny.

"The kid wants you to shut your face," he says, but the man with the tattoo is angry.

"What the hell are you playing at?" he says, taking a step closer until he is just centimetres away from me and I can smell the sweat on his clothes and the beer on his breath. But this is what I want.

I grab the can from his hand and shove him away so that he stumbles into his friend. Then I shake the can and point it at him so they are sprayed with beer. Then I drop the can and run down the platform.

Within moments they are chasing me but we are only thirty metres away from Dad and the platform is busy. Heads turn. Space closes. I feel shoulders hard against mine and people stare. I can hear the men swearing and shouting behind me and now the police officers have turned to see what is going on. The man with orange hair is still about ten paces behind me so I slow and twist my shoulder so that my bag swings around into my arms. I wait until I am almost at the uniformed officer and then I stop dead.

Orange Hair crashes into my back and I tumble to the ground, spilling my bag next to Dad's. Two of the policemen grab the men following me and block their path.

"What's going on here?" the first officer shouts. Dad stares at me for a moment, then looks away and shuffles backwards, dragging the men holding his arms with him.

"That little..." Orange Hair starts but then he thinks better of it. He is surrounded by policemen, chasing a boy across a busy station. He looks at his friend, who has beer down his shirt and is staring at me with fury on his face. Then he turns back to the policeman.

"Nothing," he mumbles.

I scramble to my feet then reach down to pick up the bag in front of me. "He barged into me," I say. "Said I spilled his drink then chased me."

"That's rubbish!" screeches Orange Hair, but everyone's watching and he's not going to do anything.

The uniformed officer stares at me, like he's got enough problems to deal with, then turns to the two plain-clothed police officers detaining Dad.

"You want me to do something?" he says.

One of them is older than the other, with grey hair

and a blue jacket, and I wonder if I've seen him before. He looks frustrated at the disturbance and he shakes his head.

"We need to deal with the suspect," he says. "Put the kid on his train then get back to the station." Then he starts to lead Dad away, before barking at the younger officer to pick up Dad's bag. She steps past me, then leans down to pick up my Adidas rucksack before throwing it to another officer, who looks inside it. I hold my breath and pray they don't realise what I've done.

"Just clothes," he says.

The woman looks at Dad. "Planning on going away for a few days?"

Dad shakes his head. "Let's just get this done," he says, pulling roughly at the cuffs and moving away down the platform.

As they go past, the older man speaks again. "Why'd you do it, Graham?" he asks, and I wonder if his tone is kind of sad. "All these years working together, I thought I knew you."

Dad's voice is bitter. "You do know me, Chris," he says. "But something stinks about all this. Where did your information come from tonight? Why were you waiting outside for me?"

"That doesn't matter," the other man said. "Now, where are they, Graham?"

"Where's what?"

"You know we'll search you, your car and your house. We know you went there this evening. You might as well tell us now."

But whatever they are talking about is in the bag I've got in my hands and Dad doesn't reply.

The officers look at each other. "Fine," the older one says. "Take him down to the station and get him booked in."

Then they drag him away.

I stare after my dad but he doesn't turn back. I am standing on a platform with nothing except a train ticket, some keys, an envelope and God-knows-what in this tin. The more I think about it, the more every fibre of my body is screaming at me to get out. Anywhere, I think, as long as it is away from here. Panic is rising and I feel like I am going to lose control, so I pinch my thumb and forefinger together like the counsellor showed me and try to breathe. There are policemen all around me so I can't just run, but I can feel the pressure in my shoulders and my jaw is clenched. Close your eyes for a moment, then open them and pick out something green, she said. Now name it in your head. *A woman's shirt.* Close your eyes again for a second and pick out something yellow. *The line on the floor in front of the train.* The writing on the station sign is brown.

It is better than counting to ten. And I have calmed before I get to blue.

The train that pulled in is still on platform two, waiting with its doors closed. A guard walks up to the policeman nearest me.

"You want me to keep holding the trains?"

The uniformed officer looks around then shakes his head. "No," he said. "Let them go."

He turns to me. "You OK now, son?" he asks.

I nod. "I need to get home," I mumble, and I walk towards platform two.

I glance over my shoulder but they aren't watching me. The police are grouped together staring back down the track. I step up to the train and I get on.

And I keep moving.

As soon as I am on the train I dart to my left, running down the aisle, pulling off my hoodie and shoving it into the bag before slapping at the button for the interconnecting doors and swerving around the other passengers until I am at the next exit. I jump down and cross the platform, walking fast, looking away from the police, over to the Brighton train, mingling among the people still getting off and on after the delay. I step up and stand next to a woman who has taken out her phone and is telling someone about the criminal she has just seen arrested, feeling the word spread out and fill the air around me. I glance through the doors at the platform clock and realise it has only been an hour since I woke up. It has all passed in a blur and I hardly have any idea what is going on.

I just know Dad was desperate to keep this tin from the police and now I'm the only who can do it. "There's always a way," he said before. "And if one of us can't do it the other one will." As the train starts to move, I wonder if he was right.

And quite how bad things might get if he wasn't.

TUESDAY
1.09 a.m.

The train is busy. The foreign students fill the carriage and make too much noise, so I head into the next compartment and find a single seat next to a large man in a dark-blue suit who is asleep. As I sit down, he grunts and shifts, sprawling further across my seat, but I push my shoulder against his and he twists away from me. He opens an eye and looks at me briefly, then closes it again and goes back to sleep.

I pull the black bag tight into my chest and I can feel the hard metal edges of the tin sharp against my ribs. Dad said he just needed a few days so that's what I'll give him, even if I need to sleep on the beach. But I need to know what's in this tin and I can't open it here. Diagonally across from me a woman stops tapping on her phone, raising her head and catching my eye before looking away again. I have a horrible sense that everyone is watching me and I don't even know what Dad was prepared to risk everything for. I need to get somewhere private as soon as I can.

Ahead of me, at the end of the carriage, is an illuminated toilet sign and I stare at it, willing it to turn off. Eventually it does and I stand quickly, making my way through the swaying compartment, determined to reach it before anyone else. I get there almost before the woman inside has had a chance to come out and then I am past her with the door closed. Inside there is a sink with a small mirror above it. I lean forward and breathe for what feels like the first time in hours.

I stare at my reflection and realise that I look like I've just got out of bed. My long fair hair is tangled and messy, falling across my dark-blue eyes, which are still sticky with sleep. The collar of my shirt is twisted, half up and half down, so I straighten it and put my hoodie back on. I look at myself again. A thirteen-year-old kid on his own on a train at night. I wonder if I stand out. I hope not, but it's too late now anyway. It's time to find out what's in this tin.

I take it out of the bag and shake it. There is a muffled rattle but no clue to the contents so I sit down on the lavatory seat and put the tin on my knees. I take a deep breath, dig my fingernails under the metal lid and rip it off.

A thick felt cloth bag bulges inside so I pull open the drawstring and tip the contents out into my hand. Inside is a rectangular box made from stained walnut wood that looks seriously old. It is about fifteen centimetres long with three faded gold initials on the top, AJR, and it has a lock like I have never seen before.

The keyhole is inlaid with silver in an elaborate pattern and looks like it is made for a five-pronged, star-shaped key, but when I tip the velvet bag up there is nothing else inside. I remember the keys Dad asked me to find and pull them out of my pocket but they are clearly a set of house keys that are far too big for this lock. I need to get into the box, but the longer it's taking the more this feeling of dread is growing. I pull out my case of dentist tools. I will have to do this the hard way.

I select one of the excavators with a bent metal prong on the end, thin enough to get into the lock, then I insert it and twist it, looking for the bite as it finds the catch mechanism. But there doesn't seem to be one. I take out another tool with a slightly thinner prong and insert them at the same time to see if the whole keyhole has to turn, but again there is nothing. I remove the tools and stare at the box in frustration.

It looks too precious to smash and I haven't got the tools here to get into it another way. I am just about to give up when I turn it over in my hand. The back of the box is the same as the front – old, faded walnut wood with two small silver hinges protruding slightly from where the lid joins the case. Except a box this finely made wouldn't have the hinges sticking out, even if they are made of silver, and suddenly I realise the whole lock is a trick. The hinges are tiny but I manage to press them both down with my thumbnails and the lid springs open with a click. I open the box and stare inside.

And wish I hadn't.

Flashes of light flicker around the dirty grey toilet, dazzling my eyes. I jerk backwards, suddenly aware of how fast my heart is beating. Inside the box is a necklace with a simple gold chain and six huge diamonds. Each diamond is cut in a distinctive rectangular shape that seems to radiate light into the small space around me. They are cold and beautiful and perfect and I recognise them instantly. These are the square diamonds of Madagascar, and my mother was wearing them the last time I saw her.

Questions fly through my mind. It's impossible, isn't it? After all that has happened! Dad hates this necklace. He says it's cursed and should be destroyed. Why would he be hiding it from the police and why are they chasing him for it?

I can't look at it, so I put the necklace back in the box and close the lid before twisting to retrieve the envelope from my pocket. The papers inside look like they've been torn from a police notebook and when I turn them over I see a list of what looks like names in Dad's small, neat handwriting.

J.M. Greenwich	Eileen Snow
Peter Black	G. Gordon
Melrose	W.M. Fox
Radcliffe's	

Somewhere in the back of my mind I have a feeling I have seen or heard one or two of these names before, but I can't recall where so I turn to the second page, which is a letter written in a rushed scrawl.

I haven't got time to write much. These people are smart so watch out.

No one knows about the house except me and that's how it should stay. The electricity, telephone, broadband, council tax and everything else is paid for. If you're careful you will be safe.

If you've kept your side of things my lawyer reckons the worst I'll get is six months. If you haven't, you'd better stay out of my way.

Taylor

I lean against the wall and read it twice because the last paragraph fills me with dread. Dad mentioned someone called Taylor in the car but some lawyer talking about six months means he must be a criminal. I wonder if Dad has been working with him, maybe even bringing him the necklace. And who are the smart people? Does he mean the police? Is that why Dad doesn't want to speak to them?

The two house keys are attached to a simple ring that has a brown label and an address: *17 Stevenson Close, Brighton*. I am not sure if it is the house in the letter but it can't be a coincidence that Dad wanted to get this train. I figure this address is where he was taking us.

Suddenly I am disturbed by a hard knock on the door.

"Come on," a voice calls. "I've been waiting bloody ages."

It jolts me. I wonder how long I have been in here. The train has stopped once, I think, so it can't have been too long, but now I need to move. I put everything back in the tin and push the lid down firmly, before standing quickly. I splash some water on my face and take a deep breath, but before I can open the door the voice calls out again.

"Come on! I'm bursting. What you doing in there?"

The demand seems to crush my mind. I need to get out, away. Somewhere I can think. I reach for the release button and open the door.

Only to come face to face with the orange-haired man I covered with beer on the station platform.

It takes him a moment to work out who I am and when he realises, his expression turns nasty. I try and take a step backwards but there is nowhere to go. He leans forward, then burps in my face before laughing. His breath is disgusting and I reach up to push him away but I've still got my bag in my hand.

"My lucky day," he says, and he pulls back his hand as if to hit me, laughing when I flinch.

I take another step back and I am inside the toilet now. My eyes flick across to the lock, but the man has jammed his foot in the doorway. He grins, then reaches out to grab me, but I bring the bag up and he hits that, crying out as his palm connects with the tin. And that makes him really angry.

He pushes me hard and I crash into the toilet. I can't draw attention to myself so I don't shout for help. I just edge back and hold the bag in front of me while he shuts the door. There is no room in the cubicle and he leans over me, shoving the bag away. I push it back between us, but he grabs at me again, reaching out to hit me. His palm connects with my face. There is a flash of light behind my left eye then a stinging pain. He pulls back his fist to strike again.

But suddenly I just let the anger out.

My heart is pounding and all the frustration and fear of the night feels like it is going to burst out of me. As his hand reaches out, I swing the bag over my shoulder and twist my body away from him. In the same movement, I grab his arm with my left hand and use his momentum to drag it downwards, towards the floor. He is caught by surprise and now he is off balance. His head smashes into the base of the toilet and I force my right hand down on to his right shoulder, pushing him to the ground, twisting his arm behind his back. It's another one of the million police things Dad showed me, but I never thought I would need to use it. He moans and I shove on his arm before letting the pressure off a little. There is blood pouring from his nose and he looks beaten. I hold his gaze for a moment then hit the button to release the door.

I am panting, trying to control my temper. I straighten up and let him go, waiting for him to spring up and attack me again, but he doesn't. He just looks away and moans in pain.

"Stay away from me," I say, then I turn to go back to my seat. I step out of the door, almost bumping into the man's friend, who is waiting outside. He stares at me, then at the guy on the floor, and takes a step backwards to let me go past. He doesn't say anything and nor do I.

I keep my head down as I march back to my seat. The sleeping man has stretched out his legs into my space. I nudge him again, hard, and he turns his back to me, leaving me perched on the edge of my seat. Then the train slows and an announcement rings out.

"*This is the Southern service to Brighton. The train is now approaching Haywards Heath. Please take all of your belongings with you when you leave the train. Thank you for travelling with Southern.*"

Several men and women get up and move towards the ends of the carriage, ready to get off. The man I am next to has put his ticket on the lowered tray table in front of him and I can see that it is for Haywards Heath. For a moment I think about letting him sleep but then I wonder who might be waiting for him and I reach across and shake his shoulder.

"Time to get up," I say. "It's a long walk home from Brighton."

The man opens his eyes and sits upright, staring around him. I stand to let him up and he joins the line of people getting off. Then the electronic chimes ring out again and I expect the automated message to be repeated, but it isn't. This time the guard's voice sounds through the speaker.

"*If Archie Blake is travelling on this train, could he please make himself known to a member of the Southern staff. I repeat. Could Archie Blake please make himself known to a member of train staff or contact a member of the police who will be joining the train. Thank you."*

When they speak my name, it's like an electric shock flashes through me. I throw myself into the seat and stare out of the window. At the end of the platform where the ticket barriers guard the exit, two police officers are carefully checking the passengers as they get off. One of them says something to the other then walks towards the train. I shrink back in the chair and cover my face with my hand as she walks past the window towards the front. I wonder if I can get off and make a run for it, but the officer at the barriers has been joined by two more. They are looking for me so I can't get off now and I haven't got time to make a plan. I have to stay trapped on the train.

The doors beep and shut, then the train starts moving slowly. The police officer got on at the front so I probably have a couple of minutes before she reaches me. I need to make a decision.

I am not ready to give myself up. My head is spinning too wildly and the look of fear in my dad's eyes is too fresh in my memory. I need to get somewhere I can breathe and that's not going to happen if I'm caught. If I sit still the officer might not notice me but that seems pretty unlikely. Maybe I can hide somewhere, but I'm pretty sure they'll check the toilet and there doesn't seem to be anywhere else. I realise I am gripping the tin through the bag as hard as I can, so I go through the exercise and force myself to be calm.

The train logo is green. The woman's phone case is yellow. The man outside has a coat that is brown...

I watch him walking slowly along the platform towards the barriers, still half asleep, with the coat getting tangled as he pulls it around him, and an idea comes to me. Perhaps I don't need to find a place to hide. Perhaps there's another way.

The speaker rings out again. "*This is the Southern service to Brighton. The next stop is Brighton, where this train terminates.*"

I stand and look around the carriage, which is still busy but dotted with empty seats, then walk slowly towards the back of the train, scanning the passengers and the luggage racks as I go. Near the front of the second carriage a businessman is slumped forward, fast asleep with his long brown coat folded neatly in the rack above him. I glance around but the other passengers are either all asleep or engrossed in their mobile phones. I move slowly towards the man, pausing as I reach him to lean on the back of his seat. Then, as calmly as I can, I stretch up and take the coat.

I carry it towards the door of the next carriage, determined not to look back, urging my heart to stop beating so fast as I wait for the indignant call, ready to turn and apologise for a simple mistake. But it doesn't come and I keep going. Near the end of the carriage a woman is asleep with her glasses on top of a half-finished crossword in front of her. I slow for a moment then lurch down with the sway of the train before I am up again with her glasses hidden in my hand, reaching for the button to open the sliding door. As I step through, I breathe out and slide the coat on over my shoulders.

No one has noticed.

I pull the coat on quickly, wrapping it around myself to hide my clothes and turning up the collar to hide my long hair. Two women are standing in the space where the exit doors open, laughing at something one is showing the other on her phone. They ignore me and I stand opposite them, putting my bag between my knees so that it is hidden by the coat. I put the glasses on, then peer over them into the glass of the door, staring at my reflection. But I still don't look different enough. I need to do something else.

The train is pretty clean but I run my finger along the hinge to the train door and it comes away filthy. The two women are still staring at the phone, now holding one white earphone each to an ear. They are not looking at me, so I take the glasses off for a moment and try to stand still. Dad told me once that people see bone structure because of the shadows it causes and that's how they recognise each other. He said it after he came back from a course and I told him he was being boring. But maybe now it's useful.

I rub the dirt in carefully to the side of my nose and look back in the window. It has changed how I look, making my nose look broken and making me look older. I put the glasses back on and pull the soft blue leather case of dentist tools out of my pocket, holding it with one flap open next to my ear like a phone case, with the tools squashed against my head and my hand spread over the whole thing. Then I turn and face the corner just in time to hear the door hiss as the police officer strides into the carriage.

I try and stay calm, but it is not easy. I think about Mum and how I used to help her learn lines for her amateur dramatic plays. "You've just got to make yourself the character," she used to say. "If you believe it, so will they." Then she would launch into the lines with a stupid voice or narrow sinister eyes or some weird accent that nobody could tell where it was from, making herself tall or scrunched up or fat or thin. Always different, but always still Mum. I shake my head to clear the image. And take a deep breath.

Australian is my best accent, so I go for that and force myself to speak in a light tone while trying to peer over the top of the glasses at the officer's reflection. The voice I put on sounds so fake I can't believe she doesn't come straight for me, but she doesn't, and so I keep talking.

"No, mate. I only got in two days ago. I'm still half asleep from the flight."

She is behind me now, only two paces away, staring down the aisle. I can sense her head moving as she surveys the passengers. I feel so stupid, clutching a pouch of dentist tools to my ear, trying to stop my knees shaking, concentrating on keeping my voice deep and steady. Trying not to listen to what I am saying.

"Everyone's complaining about the weather. Even when it doesn't rain." I pause and count to ten in my head, trying to go slower than my racing heartbeat, hating not being able to see properly out of the glasses. Then I laugh. "I guess the English are never happy, right?"

But the officer hasn't moved. She is still standing behind me and I turn slightly, just enough to get a bleary glance at her. She is youngish with mousy-brown hair and pale skin. Her left thumb is tucked into her stab vest while she uses her other hand to take her own phone out of her pocket. I turn away again and make another irrelevant comment but she is not listening any more.

"Yeah, Sarge, it's me," she says. "No. No sign, but we'll be in Brighton in five minutes. I haven't seen any kids on their own of his description but we'll check everyone getting off then do a full search of the train when we arrive."

She moves away and I see her reflection in the glass as she continues her journey down the train, her head moving from side to side again as she checks the passengers. She pushes the button to open the next set of doors and I feel like I want to collapse. I breathe a huge sigh of relief, ignoring the two women with the shopping, who look up at me then turn back to whatever they were looking at on the phone. I lean forward and rest my forehead on the cool glass of the doors until I think back to what she has just said. I have escaped for the moment, but things have just got worse, not better. There will be more policemen at Brighton and they will search the whole train.

I need to find a way to escape.

TUESDAY
1.46 a.m.

I move in the opposite direction to the policewoman, towards the front of the train. The woman with the crossword has woken up so I bend down as if her glasses have been knocked to the floor and place them helpfully back on the table in front of her. I shove the coat into the overhead rack a few spaces down from its owner and keep going until I am in the middle of the train. Then I find an empty double seat near the door and sit with my arm up next to my ear, hiding my face as I stare out of the window. The blackness flies past and I count down the seconds.

I can't think of a plan so I figure I will just run as soon as the door opens. I am fit and quick and I will surprise them. I will run until my lungs burst, until my legs ache and I am miles away. I am the fastest runner in my year and I will smash through the barriers and leave them all behind.

If I can escape, I can find somewhere to think and

then I can decide what to do. Maybe I can use the names on that list to work out what's going on and maybe they are people who will help. Whatever Dad was trying to do, he's not going to be able to do it from a police cell, so maybe he needs me to do more than just hide. I can't afford to get caught too so I ready myself to run.

But as we enter the station, my confidence crashes. Police officers line the platform, ready to get on at every door. More police line the row of ticket barriers. Flashing blue lights reflect into the station from the outside streets. Wherever I look there is no escape. Running is not going to work.

Other people are getting up, taking bags down from the rack and pulling on jackets. A queue forms either side of me, by the carriage door, but I ignore it and push through the people, walking fast into the next carriage towards the front of the train. At the next door there is another small queue and I reach it just as the train stops. The doors beep and a lady steps aside to let me go but again there is an officer, looking determined at the bottom of the step, ready for the passengers to get off. I ignore the door, grunting an apology to the woman, and move past her almost at a jog.

Again the announcement rings out.

"If Archie Blake is on the train, would he please make himself known to the station staff or police."

I increase my speed, feeling the panic rising inside me. I want to keep moving, but I am running out of train. I open the interconnecting door in front of me and I'm in the last carriage. But there is nowhere to go and the police are now on board. I am seconds away from being caught.

Before I get halfway to the front a woman stands and blocks my path. She has a large bag slung over her shoulder and is struggling to pull a pushchair out of the luggage rack. A small boy in a red cap, maybe two or three years old, is standing on a seat watching her. He looks unhappy, like he's just woken up, and as she releases the pushchair, he reaches up his arms to her.

"Up, Mummy, up," the boy says, but she is grappling with the bag and the pushchair and she ignores him, tipping her body to the side to keep the bag over her shoulder.

I stare around. Everyone else has got off, and at the other end of the carriage I can see a tall, uniformed officer stepping up to get on to the train. He climbs on and starts walking slowly through the rows of seats towards us.

The woman has the pushchair in front of her and is ready to move towards the door but the little boy has still got his arms out.

"I can't, darling," she says to him. "Mummy's got to carry all of this." She turns to me and flashes a tired apologetic look. I try to smile back, but she is blocking my path and I just want her to get out of the way.

The boy is too sleepy to understand. "Up, Mummy," he says again, more forcefully, stretching out his arms as far as they will go.

She turns to him. "Not now, Tommy, please," she says. "We need to get off the train. Please be a good boy for Mummy and jump down."

But the boy doesn't. He begins to cry. And then her patience seems to snap. I see her shoulders tense and her eyes close for a moment before she glares at him.

"Tommy, get down, now!" she says, the words coming out quickly and angrily. "We have to get off the train."

I hate it when she shouts. I know she is tired, and I know she has too much to carry, but Tommy doesn't understand why Mummy is shouting at him. She needs to pick him up and hold him but her hands are too full. Before I can stop myself, I have stepped forward.

"Let me help."

The woman turns sharply and looks like she is going to snap at me but then she stops herself. I squeeze past her and take the handles of the pushchair, easing them out of her grasp. Then I smile at her.

"Let me help," I say again. "I'll take this, and you carry your son."

She holds my gaze for a moment, then she nods and sighs. "There's always so much stuff," she says. She shrugs and smiles and picks the boy up, rubbing her nose into his neck and kissing him. "We've had a long day, haven't we, Tom?"

I watch her for a moment, thinking about the warm breath on his neck, trying to remember that feeling of being crushed in Mum's arms, but it was too long ago. She shuffles the bag on her shoulder and is ready to go. I rock the pushchair on to its back wheels and manoeuvre it a step at a time down on to the platform. The woman comes down the steps behind me, but instead of following, the policeman walks past. I wait for his footsteps, but when they don't follow I look back and he has moved on. And suddenly I want to laugh. The police are looking for a boy on his own and this officer has assumed we are a small family.

The woman steps on to the platform and turns to say thanks. She reaches to take the pushchair, but I don't want to give it back. Because maybe the same trick will work twice.

"It's OK," I say. "He looks pretty comfortable there." I smile at Tommy, who has his thumb in his mouth and has curled into his mother's arm. "I'll push this out for you."

The three of us make our way towards the barriers and I keep as close to the woman as I can, as if she is my mum too. Ahead, another officer watches as people pass through the barriers into the station. As we get closer the woman slows down and tries to open her bag to retrieve her ticket.

As she leans over the bag, she tips Tommy a little and his red Legoland sun hat falls on to the floor.

I grab my chance and pick it up, pushing it hard down on to my head and sticking out my tongue at Tommy, who squeals and holds out his hands for the hat. The woman finds her ticket, and I hold the hat out as if I am going to put it back on the boy's head except at the last minute, I ram it back on my own head and make the same silly face as before. Tommy laughs again and we move forward together until we are at the barriers, where more police officers wait.

A guard stands in front of them, checking tickets, and I walk up to him, but I still have the hat wedged stupidly on my head and have twisted away to stare at Tommy, who is behind me. The woman is laughing too now, perhaps relieved that the tears are gone, and she has her tickets in her hand.

I hold my ticket out to the guard. "Would you open the barrier, please?" I say, pushing the ticket towards him. "Mum needs to get the pushchair out."

I know the guard is looking at me, but I keep facing Tommy, making stupid faces and focusing entirely on his bright, smiling eyes. Then I sense the gate opening and without looking I move through it. The woman follows and we walk on. Five metres past the barriers, then ten, and then we are at the station exit, which leads to the taxi rank. Except just when we have reached the exit to the street, a deep voice calls out.

"Hold on, son."

I am so close. I thought I had made it. I tense my

muscles to run and the voice rings out again.

"Son. Hold on."

Slowly I turn around. It is one of the police officers, looking straight at me.

"Your brother dropped this," he says, holding out a little blue sock that Tommy has kicked off.

The woman starts to speak. "He's not—"

But I interrupt. "Thanks," I say a little too loudly, over the top of her. "One bare foot's not a very cool look, now, is it, Tom?" I say with a smile, leaning forward to take the sock before turning back round.

The woman stares at me, but I ignore her and carry on, crouching down to slip the sock on to the boy's foot before sweeping the Legoland hat off my head and holding it out to him. He grabs it and jams it on to his head then fixes his big brown eyes on me.

I lean down and straighten the hat. "Thanks, Tom," I whisper. "I owe you one." I wink and Tommy's serious look turns to a big grin. "Ice cream's on me next time," I say, and then I stand up.

Tommy's mum smiles at me. "Thanks," she says.

I shrug. "No problem."

I stare past her to the police officer, who is looking back into the station. Then I nod one more time at the woman and move on to the street.

The taxi rank is next to the car park and I am relieved to see a line of four cars waiting for passengers. I could keep walking but I don't know where I'm going and I just want to get out of here. A tired-looking woman in a business suit gets into the first car and I jump into the back of the second.

The driver is about fifty years old with thinning fair hair and a thick northern accent.

"Where to, son?" he asks.

I pat the pocket with my wallet in it, wondering how much I can afford and where the hell I'm going. Then I lean back in the seat.

"Head for the beach for now," I say, almost automatically.

Because it's time to get lost.

TUESDAY
1.53 a.m.

I shouldn't have taken a taxi.

It takes me about a minute before I realise it, and I'm kicking myself. "Criminals always leave a trail," Dad said once when he was buzzing after making an arrest. "Friends, family, cashpoints, taxi drivers. They make mistakes," he added. "That's why they always get caught."

For a moment, I wonder what mistake he made and then I wonder what he would say about me getting a taxi so obviously. But I already know because he says the same thing all the time. "Make it right," he would say. "If you make a mistake, put it right," and I can almost hear his voice in my ears.

But sometimes it's easier said than done.

Within a minute we turn a bend and I can see the sea, down a hill with the pier at the bottom, lit up by hundreds of yellow bulbs that burn bright against the black water.

"Have you got a map?" I ask.

We stop at lights and the driver turns and gives me a strange look.

"I've got a satnav," he says, which is pretty obvious because it's stuck to the middle of the windscreen, but I just shrug.

"I'm not sure of the exact address."

He rummages in his glove box and pulls out an old, stained map book, passing it over his shoulder to me. Above me there is a light and I turn it on before flicking to the back of the book to find Stevenson Close. We are moving now, down the hill, and he is wondering which way to go. There is only one Stevenson Close so I turn to page twenty-four and find square E6. It seems to be a few miles outside the centre of town in a small suburb.

"Rottingdean," I say. "Is that far?"

"Far enough."

"How much will it cost?"

"About fourteen pound."

We stop again and he turns, this time staring at me full in the face. I think about turning the light off, but it's too late. He takes a moment to look at me, as if trying to make a judgement.

"You got enough money?" he asks.

I nod. "Yeah. Take me to Rottingdean."

There was ten pounds change from the train ticket and I've got some more in my wallet but fourteen pounds is most of what I've got. And I don't know where I'm going, so I don't seem to have much choice. The car moves forward and turns left when it reaches the sea. I look back at the map and trace a route to a road a couple of streets from Stevenson Close.

"Wilkinson Avenue," I say. The driver nods, and I turn the light off.

After about fifteen minutes we turn away from the sea into a small high street. A minute later the taxi turns left, then slows down.

The driver turns to look at me. "This is Wilkinson Avenue. Where do you want?"

"Just here is fine, please," I say, and I get out.

I've got a ten-pound note, a five, three pounds and some change. I hand him the ten and the five notes and wait as he gives me a pound coin and a card with his number.

"In case you need me again," he says. And then he is gone.

I stand alone on a deserted street. It is after two

in the morning and the buzz from escaping the police has worn off. I'm starting to feel cold, which means I'm tired, and I need to get these diamonds somewhere safe. I turn out of Wilkinson Avenue, then on to the main road, then walk up the hill for about two hundred metres. Then I turn left and go past an unlit Chinese restaurant and a hairdresser until the road bends again. After another hundred metres or so I turn left into Stevenson Close.

It is a curved cul-de-sac of nondescript two- or three-bedroom semi-detached brick houses, dimly lit by two streetlamps. Number seventeen is joined to number sixteen at the peak of the road, and although it is the same structure as all the others, it is easy to tell apart. The garden is scruffy, the windows are filthy and it is set back slightly at an angle, pointing away from the other houses. The paint is peeling on the windows and several of them look rotten. It is a mirror image of the house next door except that one is clear from dirt and neglect. It looks almost as if number seventeen is trying to stay apart from the other houses in the road, and a large hedge across the front hides it even more.

There are no lights on, no cars in the drive,

no children's toys outside or any other signs of habitation. All the curtains are drawn and everything is silent. It seems empty and the letter said no one knew about it, but as I stare at it I can feel the ice in my stomach again. But there is nowhere else to go. I take a deep breath and walk as quietly as I can up the shared drive.

No one stops me. I press the white plastic doorbell and listen to the loud chime echo around the house, but there is no sign of activity. I ring it again in case there are people inside asleep, but there is still no reply, so I try the larger key in the lock and it turns smoothly. Finally I twist the handle, open the door and go inside.

I shut the front door and stand in darkness for a minute listening to the eerie emptiness of the house, waiting for my eyes to get used to the gloom. Nothing stirs so I go into the living room, which is deserted. Despite the cold I can feel the sweat on my neck and the tension in my shoulders. Slowly, silently, I go through each room then creep up the stairs. The first bedroom is empty and I crawl into the second bedroom.

A movement startles me and I leap backwards.

Within moments I am back down the stairs and at the door, but nothing follows. I listen hard but there is no sound. I wait thirty seconds but there is still nothing. Fear is screaming in every cell of my body, but I need to know if there is someone in the room.

I creep up the stairs again and open the door... And see my reflection in the full-length mirror. I slump against the wall and wonder how I could have been scared of myself. There is no one in the house and I am alone. Wearily I get to my feet and go downstairs, making sure the curtains are all closed before turning on a lamp to look around.

The house is full of stuff but it doesn't feel like a home. I try and work out why, then realise it's because there are no personal possessions anywhere. There's a telephone table with no telephone, coat hooks with no coats. In the living room it is the same. A bookcase with no books, a mantelpiece with no photos and a TV in the corner that isn't plugged in. At the rear of the living room is a dining area and then there's a door to the kitchen, which stretches across the back of the house. There is crockery in the cupboards but nothing in the fridge, and on the wall there is a clock powered by a dying battery so that it ticks slowly and intermittently. As I look around, I realise the house is just home to furniture, dust and a heavy silence broken only by the drunken rattle of the clock's second hand as it tries but fails to move from one number to the next.

I guess I was kind of hoping there would be people here who knew what was going on, but it doesn't look like anyone's been here in ages. I lock the front and back doors, trying to shake off the strange fear of being trapped as I do; leaving the keys in the locks so they can't be opened from the outside without giving me some warning of anyone trying to get into this place. Then I head to the smaller bedroom and dump my stuff on one of the two beds before slumping down wearily on to the other.

I kick off my shoes but leave on my other clothes, then get into bed, lying awake in the darkness and listening to the night-time whisperings of the house, trying to run through what Dad said in the car but it is already fading.

I almost found them, but they were expecting me. I just need a few days.

I can't remember the rest. All I can think about is the fear in Dad's eyes and the horrible dread I had when he didn't come home. "Criminals always get caught," he once said, "so there's nothing to worry about."

Unless you're the one who's committed the crime.

What trouble is Dad really in?

I close my eyes but the thoughts whir around in my head until finally sleep comes.

TUESDAY
9.26 a.m.

A noise.

I lurch out of bed. The tin is in my hand, my bag is over my shoulder and my shoes are on. Panic floods through me as a car door thumps and I am by the kitchen door, ready to run, watching through the hall window as a figure approaches the house. Except when they reach the door another opens and slams and I realise they have gone into next door. My heart is pounding and I slump to the floor and try to calm myself. The tiles behind the sink are green. The clock is yellow. The cupboard doors are brown...

I can hear the person move through next door, in a bad mood, slamming the door then stamping loudly into the kitchen before I hear the tap run and the thump of a kettle banged down on to its power point. Then a rattle of keys as they unlock the back door and march out into the garden.

I want to know who it is so I keep as quiet as I can

and creep up the stairs, into the main bedroom at the rear of the house, crouching down and moving to the window that looks out on to the back garden. Then when I raise my head and peer out past the frayed yellow curtains I can see them clearly.

It is a girl, about my age, dressed in a black T-shirt, trainers and jeans, with blonde hair pinned back behind her head. She is carrying a steaming cup of tea or coffee and she sits at an old picnic table in the garden, staring at her phone, swiping at the screen quickly as if she is looking for something specific. Until she seems to find it and watches carefully for about a minute. When she reaches the end, she seems to relax a little and pauses to take a sip from her cup.

But it is still too hot. As she takes the sip she cries out and jerks back as if stung by the heat of the drink, spilling some of it down her shirt and on to the table. She jumps up, scalded a second time, and runs into the house. I stand too, surprised by the sudden movement, craning to see what she is doing until she comes out again a few seconds later, dabbing a cloth on to a small brown stain on the front of her shirt. I look away for a moment, surprised at the intensity of the small drama.

And when I look back she is staring straight at me.

For a moment our eyes lock. She is shocked; staring at me as if I am a monster. Her large green eyes are wide and her mouth is slightly open. A second goes past and then another and her eyes don't leave me. Then slowly her expression changes and I can see she isn't scared or angry, she is confused. She is just staring at me, keeping perfectly still, working out what to do.

And then she moves.

Her eyes are still fixed on mine but her hand reaches for her phone and the tension snaps. I charge out of the bedroom and down the stairs into the kitchen, twisting the key in the lock and wrenching the door open, bursting into the overgrown garden without thinking. The fence between the two houses is low and I see her scrolling through her phone searching for a number. I shout for her to stop but she ignores me, raising the phone to her ear. Next to the fence there is an old white plastic chair and I run up and step on to it, pulling myself over and into her garden. And now we are face to face.

As I land, she starts running towards the house, but I am too quick and get between her and the open door. I just need to talk to her before she makes a call, but now she is scared and she backs away from me, holding her arms out defensively.

"Don't make that call," I say, edging towards her.

She glares at me. "Who the hell are you?" she says in a rough, angry voice, spitting the words at me. "Get the hell out of my garden."

I hold up my hands. "I'm from next door," I say. "We've just moved in."

She raises the phone to her ear, backing away quicker now, shaking her head. "Rubbish!" she shouts.

"It's true," I say. We are almost at the back of the garden. There is nowhere left to go. "Please put your phone down." I try to smile but she isn't buying it.

"You're a liar," she spits.

The phone connects as she reaches the rear fence. I see her breathe in as if she is about to speak and I know I can't let that happen. Running forward, I barge her into the fence. I reach for her arm as we struggle and I grab her hand, squeezing it hard, then ripping the phone from her grip. I back away fast and disconnect the call. She is standing a few metres away from me, breathing heavily, and her eyes are filled with rage.

"Give me my phone back," she shouts.

I can feel myself edging backwards, shocked at what I have done. "I'm sorry," I say. "I didn't mean to attack you."

"Who the hell are you?" she says.

"I told you. We just moved in."

"Liar."

"It's true," I say, except I think *we both know it's not*. I frantically try and come up with a name. "My name's Smith," I say. "Archie Smith."

She almost laughs. "Yeah, right! Now, give me my phone back."

I look down at the phone in my hand before looking back up at her. The last number she called is still on the screen but there is no name next to it.

"This is a mobile number," I say, "not the police. Who were you calling?"

"None of your business. Now, give me my phone and tell me who you really are."

She raises her clenched fists and stares at me. The fear has gone and there is just anger in her eyes. I don't want to fight. I hold out my hands to reason with her.

"My name's Archie Smith," I insist. "We're renting the house. We moved in last night. I thought you might think I was a burglar."

She just snorts. "That's enough," she says. "Even if that is your name, you're lying about living here. My dad owns that house and he hasn't rented it to anyone. Now, give me back my phone."

As she speaks, she takes a big step towards me, raising her right fist. Her whole body has tensed and suddenly I get the impression she knows what she's doing. I raise my hands to block her punch but it doesn't come. Instead she throws her left hand into the air. I twist to block that but then she steps forward and brings her knee up as hard as she can. And I am practically blinded by the pain.

"You shouldn't mess with a girl if you don't know who her dad is, Archie Smith," she whispers, then she steps back while I collapse to the ground. The phone falls from my hand on to the grass and she crouches to pick it up.

I groan and try to stand but the pain is too much and I feel sick. She raises the phone to call again.

"Wait," I gasp. "I do know who your father is."

She looks down on me and I can see the contempt on her face. "Liar," she says again, but her eyes don't leave mine.

"This time it's true," I say, struggling to sit up. "I've got a note from him." I push myself back against the fence and breathe deeply. "His name's Taylor."

She holds my gaze for a long time before nodding slowly and lowering the phone. "All right," she says. "Show me the note. But if you try anything else, there's more where that came from."

It takes me a minute to recover enough to climb back over the fence to number seventeen and the girl follows. I sit down heavily at the kitchen table and hand her the letter.

She reads it, then looks up at me suspiciously. "Your name's not Smith," she says. "It's Blake, isn't it?"

Panic flows through me and I feel like I've been stung. I stumble to deny it, but she turns the phone towards me to show me what she was looking at.

"You need to stop lying, Archie!" she says. "Your description's all over social media. Your dad's Graham Blake, isn't he?"

I don't speak but I can feel my shoulders slump. I pick up the phone and scan over the YouTube page she has opened. Her key words are "Arrests Art and Antiques unit," and top of the results is a video of a police press conference where a senior-looking officer is standing outside a police station talking reluctantly to a group of noisy journalists. When I open the video, he starts to speak.

"*Further to a huge amount of online speculation, I can confirm that Detective Inspector Graham Blake of the Art and Antiques unit of the Metropolitan Police was arrested last night trying to board a train to Brighton and is now being held on suspicion of attempted robbery. We know the public expect its police to behave with absolute integrity and therefore we are extremely disappointed to find ourselves in this position. As this is an active investigation, I can't say any more at this point other than to add that we are also looking for Archie Blake, who is missing. He is described as thirteen years old, white, six feet tall, with shoulder-length blond hair and blue eyes, wearing a red T-shirt, a blue hoodie and jeans. Naturally, as the boy is on his own, we are concerned for his safety and appeal for him to contact the police as soon as he can. A further statement will be issued in due course.*"

As the officer stops, the journalists start shouting out questions. Someone says something about corruption in the Met. Then a woman calls out louder than the others.

"*Is it true that the famous Madagascan diamonds have been stolen?*" she shouts. "*Can you confirm whether you've recovered the necklace yet?*"

But the officer doesn't reply. "*No more questions,*" he barks. And then he hurries back into the building.

I stare at the screen and that tiny hope buried somewhere inside me that this has all been some sort of messed-up game finally dies. It is real and it is happening now. Dad has been arrested for theft and the police are looking for me. I slide the phone back across the table and the girl picks it up.

She shrugs. "A load of diamonds go missing and you end up in a house owned by Tony Taylor. I think it's time you dropped the act, don't you?"

There doesn't seem to be any point pretending any more. I nod my head. "Yes," I say. "I'm Archie Blake." I stare at her. "Are you going to call the police?"

But she just laughs. "Call the police here," she says. "My dad would disown me! If you want to hand yourself in that's fine with me, but I won't be calling them."

A thought hits me. "I haven't got the diamonds," I say quickly.

But she just pushes back her chair and stands up. "And there was me feeling lucky."

We stare at each other before she reaches up and adjusts one of the grips in her hair. "Wait here," she says. "I'm going to get my tea."

A few minutes later she comes back but with two cups in her hands. She puts one in front of me.

"You can drink that," she says. "And then you'd better go."

I take a sip, wondering what I'm going to do now. "So what's your name?" I ask.

She looks at me, like she's trying to make up her mind whether to tell me. Then she shrugs. "Sam Bunting," she says. "People call me Bunny."

"Bunting? I thought your name was Taylor."

"My parents are divorced. This is my dad's house and I look after it when he's banged up. And you should be pretty pleased that's where he is right now because if you met him you'd run a mile."

I had assumed Taylor must be a criminal but it's still a shock to hear it and I wonder again what sort of people Dad is mixed up with. I look away and try to sound calm.

"But you went into next door?"

"He owns them both," she says. "He likes to keep things close by and everyone knows search warrants only cover one address." She stops and checks her watch. "And that's enough questions," she says. "I've got things to do." She finishes her drink and stands up. "You need to go."

I stand up too. "Why can't I stay here?" I say. "It'll just be a couple of days then Dad will come and get me."

Bunny snorts. "Come and get you," she says, shaking her head. "They've arrested him. They're not going to let him out to play, even if he gets bail. They'll rush it through, and he'll be banged up in double-quick time. That's the way it works."

She talks like it's a done deal and I am shocked. Dad can't really be guilty, can he? And if he goes to prison, what would happen to me?

"What if he hasn't done anything?" I say.

She scoffs. "What do you mean, if he hasn't—" she starts, before stopping suddenly. Her expression softens. "You wouldn't have known, though, would you? You poor kid. Hurts, don't it, when you find out?"

I stare at her. I'm thinking that I don't want to hear

this but I have to ask. "Wouldn't have known what?" I say.

"That he's bent, what else?"

"It's not true," I say forcefully. "He's not bent. He's not corrupt. It's just some kind of mistake." But even as I say the words, I think about the necklace hidden in the tin and the doubts creep in. I remember how it sparkled the night Mum borrowed it. And how much Dad hated it. Why does he have it?

Bunny shakes her head. "Wake up, Blake," she says. "The plod wouldn't arrest one of their own unless they were sure. They certainly don't announce it to the press unless they've got evidence. It's criminals that make mistakes, not the police." Then she laughs, but without humour.

"And why would he be dealing with my dad?" she adds. "Tony Taylor's been a crook all his life and precious stones are what he knows best. You need to get used to it. Your dad's been caught. And life's going to be a lot tougher from now on. You need to hand yourself in and get on with it."

I don't look at her. I just stare at the table and feel the cold rise up my spine. What if she's right? What do I do then? I shake my head to try and clear it.

Bunny is still staring at me and I can feel my jaw tighten.

"I'm not giving myself up," I say.

"Got any money?"

"No."

"Then you're going to have to," she says bluntly. She shakes her head and puts the phone in her pocket. "Look," she says. "You can stay here for a few hours and get your head straight. Then you go." She crosses her arms. "Understand?"

I look at her. My head's a mess and I need to think. This is the only place I've got, so I nod. "OK," I say.

"Just don't get your hopes too high," she says. "Because they always let you down."

She looks sad for a moment then shrugs again and picks up her mug to take it back to the other house. But just before she does, I have a thought and stop her.

"Can you show me where the computer is?" I say. "I can't find one."

She looks confused. "Why d'you think there's a computer?"

"Your dad's note says the house has got broadband. I figured there must be."

"Broadband?" Bunny laughs. "It hasn't even got a telephone."

For a moment I think I may have been wrong and I check the note, but I am right. "*The electricity, telephone, broadband, council tax and everything else is paid for*," I read, then I stare at her. "So there must be a telephone line somewhere," I say. "Why don't you just tell me?"

The words come out angrily. I know she doesn't want me here, but I don't see what harm she thinks I can do by using the computer. All I want to do is look up those names and try and work out why Dad thought they were important, but it's obvious she doesn't want to help. I shove the letter into her hand, then march to the front door, open it and walk backwards, away from the house, shielding my eyes from the August sunlight as I stare up into the sky. The telegraph pole is two doors down to the right, stretching up over the height of the roofs, releasing its spider's web of wires down to each of the surrounding houses, including number seventeen.

I point to the wire that comes down into the back of the house. "You see?" I say. "There is a phone line, like the note says. We just need to find it."

I march from room to room, but I still can't see the connection. Bunny follows until we finally get to the big bedroom, but I check all the walls and there is nothing there either. The frustration is burning inside me.

"I've been trying to tell you," she starts. "There isn't a phone. He only ever uses disposable mobiles."

But I'm sure I am right and I'm not going to give up. I drag a dressing table out to the landing, then climb up and force the loft panel back into the blackness in the roof. I reach up for the light switch, but either I'm not tall enough or there isn't one. I climb into the dark, throwing my body up into the black space above. The floor is boarded so I roll back and allow the light from the hatch to spill up into the dark. I can see the walls are panelled with the same hardboard as the floor and the loft is completely enclosed. There is no light and no sign of a telephone line. And unlike our loft at home, which is full of old junk, the space is empty.

I crawl into the middle of the attic and try to work out which is the outside wall where I saw the phone line come into the house from the street. But it's strangely difficult. The side panels connect to the floor at ninety degrees with a smooth join all the way up. There are no wires running anywhere along it and the feeling of confidence that swept over me when I saw the telegraph pole has gone. Maybe I should have believed Bunny, but I don't know who she is and I don't trust her. I stop looking and sit down, wondering why I'm scrabbling around in a dark loft in a strange house. It all seems such a waste of time.

Bunny's face appears at the hatch and she looks angry.

"Happy now?" she says. "I told you there was nothing in the roof. It's you who tells lies, not me."

I don't look at her and she climbs back down. I was wrong and I hate it. I smash my palm on the flat of the floor. I am tired and fed up and I don't want to go back down to hear her tell me I how stupid I've been. The frustration bursts out and I throw myself back against the board behind me.

And the world changes.

TUESDAY
10.08 a.m.

As soon as I push back on the hardboard, it gives way and a light flicks on. I fall backwards and gasp. I am in a narrow room, about two metres wide by six metres long, just tall enough to stand in, running all the way along the side of the house. And it is completely crammed with stuff.

At one end of the room is a high-backed leather chair in front of a desk that is covered in computer equipment. Along the side wall, into the eaves of the house, is a long row of sleek dark-grey metal drawers and on the opposite wall a set of shelves covered in rows of bright-coloured plastic boxes. On the ceiling above, tools are clipped into holding brackets and at the other end of the room there is a large wardrobe. I get to my feet and gaze at it all. I was only trying to find the phone but this is something else.

When I look in the boxes I find they are all packed with kit. There are screwdrivers, metal files, hacksaws, hammers and hand-held drills. There are different-sized torches, latex gloves and ski masks; batteries of every size and shape; as well as solar chargers, pressure gauges and a series of green medical boxes stamped with a red cross containing everything from bandages to iodine. The clips on the ceiling hold larger items like bolt cutters, drills and coils of wire. There is a range of crowbars, and even a crossbow pinned above my head with bolts attached to super-strength microfibre cord. Some of it is old and it's pretty obvious none of it has been used for a while because everything is covered in a thick layer of dust.

On the desk, a screen jumps to life when I approach it, showing a bank of six video streams that are clearly being taken by CCTV cameras. Next to it is a laptop and two brand-new iPhones, sitting in chargers, with two unopened pay-as-you-go SIM cards. And next to that I finally find the phone line, plugged into a cradle for a handset and a superfast wireless router.

"Hey, Bunny," I yell. "I found your dad's secret room."

She doesn't reply so I go back to the hatch and stick my head through just as she is walking back up the stairs.

"I found it," I say again and pull her up, leading her through the darkness and back into the room. "Even though you didn't want me to."

Her face is a blank mask. "I didn't know it was here," she says quietly.

I shake my head. "You don't seem very surprised. No wonder you didn't want me to go to the police. You get caught with this stuff, you're in big trouble."

"I can't see anything illegal," she says defensively. "It's just tools and that." But we both know she's wrong.

"Not illegal?" I say. "Everything here's designed to be used in robberies!"

I walk over to the two banks of metal drawers that nestle in the eaves. At the slightest touch, the first drawer hisses smoothly open. Inside, twelve shining metal items are embedded into a cushion of grey foam. I reach out and pick up one of the flat, heavy steel tools and turn it over. One end is curved into a small claw while the paddle-shaped other end sits perfectly in the palm of my hand.

"Lock picks and tension wrenches," I murmur, more to myself than Bunny. "And skeleton keys." I put it back and open another drawer. "Single-bit microdrills with diamond tips. A compressed-air hammer, compressed-air hinge breakers, lock punches." I stop and stare at her. "Night-vision goggles, GPS trackers, micro cameras, listening devices and God knows what," I say. "There's even some plastic explosives in here. This place is unbelievable."

Her face is like stone. "Yeah, well, it seems pretty believable to me."

She moves past me to open the wardrobe at the end of the room, revealing a range of clothes and shelves of make-up. She picks up a wig absent-mindedly before replacing it and heading back towards the empty attic. Until suddenly she stops and goes back to the drawers. She opens one and looks inside, then turns to me with a puzzled look on her face.

"There are no labels on any of this stuff," she says. "How do you know what it is?"

I shrug. "I don't know," I say. "Why shouldn't I?"

She frowns and shakes her head. "No one just knows what this stuff is. And how come you recognised how some of it worked?"

Her tone of voice is accusing and I don't like it. "My dad showed me," I say. I am about to say more when Bunny grabs one of the tools from the drawer.

"Did he show you what this was?"

I nod. "It's a tension wrench. You use it to hold open a lock you're picking."

Bunny snorts. "So you know how to pick locks," she says.

"It's not hard," I say. "We have races to see who can pick them the fastest."

But she's not satisfied with that. "Show me," she demands.

I stare at her for a moment. She is standing very still and her chin is jutting out in determination. She holds my gaze without blinking and I find myself reaching up to one of the pigeonholes and taking out a simple padlock.

I push it shut before taking another tool out of the top drawer as well as the tension wrench she is holding out. They balance in my hands like they have been made for me and I hesitate, then push them into the lock, first one then the other. Then I twist.

The lock snaps open.

Bunny acts as if nothing has happened. She just reaches up to a box of bigger padlocks and tosses one to me.

"What about this?" she says.

"Why d'you choose this one?"

"You think you're the only one who knows things? Can you open it or not?"

The padlock takes a dual-sided key, which means it's harder but I can do it. I take a different tool out of the drawer and twist it into the keyhole. I grit my teeth for a moment, working hard to get purchase on the mechanism, and after a few seconds it opens.

Bunny is staring at me with wide eyes. "And your dad taught you that, did he?"

"I bet I could open anything in this room."

Bunny points at some of the other tools. "What about the rest of this stuff?" she says. "Do you know how to use that too?"

Before I can answer she's picked up what looks like a large pair of mechanical pliers with flat ends. "What's this?" she demands.

"It's for breaking the hinges on safes."

"How does it work?"

I explain. "You slide these thin parts into the space, pump this to increase the pressure then release it here. The hinges should rip right off."

"What about if the hinges are inverted?"

It's a trick question so I smile. "There aren't many

safes with inverted hinges because putting them on the outside makes them easy to get at. You wouldn't need this."

Bunny nods slowly then sits down hard in the chair. She is gazing at me, but she looks more disappointed than impressed. "And you don't think he's corrupt," she says slowly. "Why else would he show you this stuff?"

And suddenly the buzz from picking the locks is gone. The doubt hits me as I realise what she is saying.

"He's a policeman," I say. "It's his job to know this. He just showed it to me."

"There's nothing wrong with knowing stuff," she says. "He didn't need to teach you how to use it. Your dad's turning you into a criminal, Archie. Is that what you want?"

"It was just what we did," I say. "Our way of spending time together."

Bunny shakes her head. "But he's been arrested, Archie. You need to grow up and see what's going on."

She looks at me like I'm some kind of innocent and I feel my hackles rise. She doesn't know, does she? She doesn't realise how hard it was to sit there every day in silence. I can feel my triggers growing inside me and I force my fingers to relax.

"Don't tell me what to do," I say quietly. "It's nothing to do with you."

But she just doesn't let up. "Like hell it isn't," she spits. "If you bring the police here, what do you think that means for my dad?"

"It's his stuff," I say, and I can hear my voice getting louder. "Maybe he deserves whatever he gets."

Bunny takes a step towards me. "Who the hell are you to judge anyone?" she snarls. "If you bring the police here, I'll rip your bloody head off."

"So it will be my fault, will it?" I say angrily. "Your dad's the one in jail, not mine."

"Sounds like they both will be soon," she yells back. "And where's your mum in all this mess? Looks like she saw sense and dumped you too."

And then the fury just bursts out of me. "What the hell do you know?" I scream. "My mum's dead, all right, so why don't you just get out of my face."

I can't stop the words, even though I do my best to never say them. Because I don't talk about it. I spend most of the time trying not to think about it, even when it seems like it is the only thing I will ever think about again. I am so tired of wondering why my life has been smashed apart, but every time those words are said, it feels like I've lost another tiny piece of the wreckage. And every piece lost means I will never be able to put things back together.

Now I am shouting at the top of my voice and feel ready to smash this whole place up too. Until I see the look of fear on Bunny's face.

She has taken a step back, but she holds my gaze and says nothing until eventually I force myself to calm. She sighs. "I'm sorry," she says. "I didn't know. But it doesn't change much."

That's what people say, isn't it? That they're sorry, but I don't really know what it means. I don't know what they are sorry for and most of the time I don't think they do either. I don't reply. I just watch in silence as she turns, then steps towards the panel to leave the room.

Except when she reaches it, she seems to hesitate and turns back.

"Look," she says. "I don't make the rules, OK? I'm just the one who has to deal with my dad's mess. Stay for today and then go."

I don't answer and she lifts the panel to leave.

"What will you do without money?"

I almost laugh as I look at the stuff on the walls around me. "I'm sure I'll think of something."

"Archie?" Her voice is quiet.

"What?"

"I'm sorry, OK? It must be tough. But don't pin your hopes on your dad because he'll let you down. And don't do anything you'll regret."

She takes a step towards me then digs in her pocket and pulls out a twenty-pound note. "It's all I've got," she says, and puts it on the desk. Then she ducks through the panel and is gone.

I listen as she drops down out of the roof, then goes downstairs, into the kitchen and out of the back door. And once more the house is silent. Once more I am alone. I look around the room and wonder if things are better or worse.

I tell myself I don't believe Dad is guilty, but it is hard to shake off the doubt. Except I don't really understand why he would want to do it. What's he going to do with a fortune in diamonds? He's got a good job. I don't think we spend a lot. We don't go on holiday and he hasn't even fixed the dent in the car. But I don't know. And I don't have time for doubts.

I've got things to do.

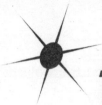

TUESDAY
10.39 a.m.

I need to eat something, which means I need to go out and that means I need to change the way I look. The police are looking for me and have probably traced me to Brighton, but they may not have got further than that yet, so I have to act now.

I get changed into the clean underwear and black T-shirt that Dad brought and cut off the bottom of my jeans to turn them into shorts. Then I try hacking at my hair to shorten it, but films make it look a lot easier than it is. I curse myself because I look ridiculous, with blond tufts sticking out everywhere, and I know I won't be able to fix it without help. In the wardrobe in the attic there were some hats so I grab a baseball cap and a pair of chunky black glasses with clear lenses, which will do for now. I put a SIM card into the new phone I'd grabbed from the attic room, then pick up the tin and stare at it for a moment before deciding to leave the diamonds in the house.

If I'm caught, I don't want the police to get them, so I need to hide them and I want them in a place that's near the door in case I have to run.

I think for a moment then go downstairs into the kitchen and shove the black velvet-wrapped box into the freezer compartment of the fridge, hesitating before slamming the door shut and turning away. Then I sling the bag over my shoulder and leave the house.

The hairdresser on the corner has one of its four chairs occupied by an older woman having her hair dried. The stylist standing behind her is about forty with dark-red hair. She's wearing a white T-shirt and jeans, and chatting with a younger blonde woman sitting on a stool behind the till. I walk past, holding my breath for as long as I can, until my face is red and my breathing heavy. Then I turn back and push open the door.

A bell rings and the girl behind the till looks up.

"Yes, love?" she says.

"Some boys did it," I stammer. "I don't know what to do."

The stylist with the dryer looks up and I can see the customer's eyes glance at me through the mirror.

The blonde girl hesitates but the older woman lowers the dryer for a moment. "What do you mean, love?" she says.

I take off my hat. "They held me down," I say. "I don't know what to do. I've got some money."

They are staring at me. The customer in the chair looks shocked. "Go to Hightown School, do you?" she asks.

I shrug and the women seem to look at each other. "Can you do something?" I say, then repeat, "I've got some money."

The lady with the red hair walks over to the girl at the till and runs her finger down the page of the reservations book in front of her. "Mrs Bangla's not due in for half an hour," she says. "You could do something, couldn't you, Trace?"

Trace looks shocked. "Not sure how much I can do with that, Mrs S," she says, walking over to me. She pulls at a tuft of my hair, which comes out in her hand. "We could cut it all off, I suppose."

But Mrs S is on my side. "We can do better than that," she says. She stands next to Trace and runs her fingers through my hair. "Cut it short but see if you can do something with the top." She winks at me.

"Don't worry, love, you're a handsome boy and we'll soon have you looking better than ever."

I breathe a sigh of relief loud enough for them all to hear and smile at her then dig into my pocket to pull out a fistful of change. "I've got some money," I say, but Mrs S shakes her head. "You keep your money," she says. "Trace's got time. It will be a challenge."

The customer in the chair nods. "Quite right, Steph," she says. "Those boys from Hightown get out of control in the holidays. It's about time they did something about it."

It feels strange, running my hands through short hair. For a moment a memory flashes in my head of Mum doing it when I was little. That warm, tickly feeling on my scalp as she strokes my hair with soft fingers and smiles. But it doesn't last long. The memory is too brief to cling to and I am alone again.

On the small Rottingdean high street there are several charity shops as well as a baker, a florist, a convenience store and a dry cleaner. I look in a charity shop for new clothes but they are more than I want to spend and I can feel the assistant's eyes on me. I turn around quickly and leave the shop just as a blue

Mercedes 4x4 bumps up on to the pavement a few metres down.

A man gets out, carrying two suits on hangers, and dashes into the dry cleaner's. Because his car is blocking half the pavement, I have to wait while a lady in a mobility scooter drives slowly through the gap and I watch through the window as he hands over the suits and takes a small green ticket from the woman inside. Then he comes out and jumps into his car while the lady takes the suits into the back room then returns to the counter.

And now I know what I need to do.

A few buildings down is an alleyway that runs behind the shops, and I jog along it until I reach the dry cleaner's. Behind the shop is a gate to a small yard, then a back door next to a window through which I can see racks of clothes. The door is locked but the window is open to let the breeze in and from inside I can hear a radio from the front of the store, but nothing else. As slowly and silently as I can, I push the old wooden window further open then lever myself up on to the ledge and drop inside. Just then the bell rings and a customer comes into the shop.

There are several racks of clothes, but I don't

have time to look at them as the sound of the radio suddenly gets louder and the door to the shop opens. I drop to the floor and roll under one of the racks, pushing myself against the wall, hoping the rows of suits and shirts will hide me. I see the legs of the assistant walk into the room, step up to one of the other racks and take a plastic-wrapped hanger of clothes. She then turns and heads back into the shop.

I am about to roll out but she comes back almost immediately. This time she is carrying a long dress.

"When do you want it back?" she calls into the shop.

I hear another woman's voice. "It's not urgent," she says. "Sometime next week will be fine."

I see the assistant's feet turn as she looks around, then settles on the rack on the far side of the room. She takes an empty hanger from it, slides the dress over the wire and pushes a blue label with a large "M" on it over the hook.

"I'll put you down for Monday," she says. "That will be fifteen pounds twenty."

She walks back into the shop and I crawl out of my hiding place, grabbing some clothes that might fit me and are not due back until next week. Suits and shirts and a thin black sweater. For a moment, I hesitate with my hands on the hangers. I am about to steal something, and I am buzzing with energy and fear and excitement. I intend to bring them back, but I still know this is wrong. But I don't have any more time to think about it. The bell in the shop rings again and I practically throw myself out of the window.

When I get back and change, I look in the mirror and hardly recognise myself. One pair of trousers is much too wide for me and the other is slightly too short, but when I put on my trainers and roll up the legs to my ankles it looks OK, or at least deliberate. I put the glasses back on then nod my head and smile grimly. I am looking at a stranger.

Archie Blake has gone.

TUESDAY
2.25 p.m.

Bunny's twenty pounds is still intact and sits on the table together with a few coins, the house keys and the list of names from Dad's bedside table. I bought some food but when I got to the till I found that I didn't want to break into the note. I stare at it for a minute then shake the thoughts of owing Bunny out of my head before picking up the list and heading upstairs to the attic room. Dad had these names hidden so they must be important and I want to know why. I also want to know why he had the diamonds. I can't believe it's got nothing to do with what happened to Mum and a horrible feeling of unease seeps through me. Whatever the reason, I want to know what Dad was up to. I fire up the laptop, open Google and start typing in the names from the list.

J.M. Greenwich   Eileen Snow
Peter Black   G. Gordon

Melrose   W.M. Fox
Radcliffe's

By five o'clock I have keyed a thousand different combinations of these names into the search engine, with no success. I start by typing them in one by one but get millions of random results and none of them seem to mean anything. J.M. Greenwich is a microfilm business in south London, Eileen Snow is a children's writer, Peter Black is a company that sells shoes, G. Gordon is a DJ who specialises in upsetting people and W.M. Fox is an actor. Melrose is a town in Scotland and all I get from Radcliffe's is about a million images of Harry Potter.

I try putting the names in together but I get another million results that also mean nothing. Then I try all the combinations in different ways but still nothing makes any sense and I am getting nowhere. I want to scream in frustration.

Dad would tell me to be patient. Another one of his lessons in life that I ignored whenever I could. Suddenly I feel so scared I'm not going to hear him say it again that I feel cold. There were times it would make us want to scream at him.

I remember Mum getting angry with the ironing board and crashing it up and down and complaining that she was sick of it not working and we should get a new one, but all he did was get his tools and tell her to be patient. An hour later pieces of it were laid out neatly on the floor and that big pile of ironing was just sitting there on the side. Mum was standing with her hands on her hips and saying that being patient will leave us all old and grey. Then she looked at me and wagged her finger. "Don't let me catch you running up those stairs and having fun, young Archibald," she said. "You be patient like your father and take them one step at a time. By the time you get to the top, it will be time to come back down again."

She put on a silly Scottish voice to make us laugh but Dad held out his arms and looked confused and hurt at the same time. "How can it be wrong to take a little time to get things right?" he said, and Mum raised her eyes to the ceiling and groaned in frustration, then started to laugh. She pulled him into the tightest hug and told him that he drove her crazy but he'd better not change.

"If you hadn't been patient, you'd have never got me," she said to him, and she squeezed him as hard as she could. "So, Graham Blake, don't you dare ever change."

But things do change, don't they? And there's nothing we can do to stop them.

I lean back and stare at the ceiling, wondering what to do next, and as I do I notice the light from above gleaming on a set of metal bolt cutters. It reminds me of the glints of light when I first opened the walnut-wood box, and a thought strikes me. I turn back to the keyboard and type in: *J.M. Greenwich Diamonds*. There is nothing useful on any of the first fifty pages of results, but I try again. *Eileen Snow Diamonds* brings nothing but when I finally type: *Peter Black Diamonds* I find something that could be relevant two-thirds of the way down the eighth page of results.

It is an article on the website of the *Somerset County News*:

Peter Black of Taunton, West Somerset, spoke of his relief that the diamonds had not been taken. "Those diamonds have been in our family since my great-grandfather brought them back from India in 1870 and it was fortunate that the thieves didn't take them during the burglary."

Superintendent Lisa Mackenzie of the specialist Art and Antiques crime unit at the Met warned the public to be vigilant. "We think the intruders were just kids who had no idea of what they almost had. We have been lucky in this and in the break-in at Melrose Hall that on neither occasion the jewellery was removed from the premises." She was referring to the thefts in Stirling last year when thieves took a television set and a microwave but ignored a sixteenth-century ruby brooch given to Anne Boleyn by Henry VIII. When asked if she was confident of an imminent arrest, the superintendent merely repeated that the force was following its usual lines of enquiry.

I read it quickly and when it refers to Melrose Hall, I know I have found something. And Mackenzie is Dad's boss and one of the few senior officers he rates so I bet she would have told him about these cases. It must all be linked and now the time goes quicker until eventually I have linked the first six names from Dad's notes. They are all people who owned jewellery with some sort of historical significance.

J.M. Greenwich had a pair of emerald earrings that had once belonged to Princess Anne of Austria. Eileen Snow had a sapphire pendant that had been given to her grandmother by Edward VII. G. Gordon is a descendent of General Gordon of Khartoum, and the gem was a single pink diamond looted from the imperial palace of China. The Madagascan diamonds that Mum had been wearing match this profile exactly.

And what is more, all six have been the victims of crime in the last four years. Except in each instance, the jewels had either been left behind or recovered almost immediately, either through good luck, carelessness or because the robbers hadn't realised what they could have taken. Dad's unit was mentioned in four of the cases so he definitely would have known about all of them, but I don't know why he would have written them all down and kept the list hidden. None of them help me work out what's going on.

I lean back in the chair and am about to see if I can find a link to Radcliffe's when the images from the security cameras flicker into life and I see Bunny walking up the driveway. I hurry downstairs to let her in just as she starts banging on the door.

"The whole town's crawling with plod," she says, striding into the kitchen and slinging her bag on to the table. "It's not safe here. You need to go now."

"How close are they?"

She almost laughs. "Don't worry. I didn't lead them here." And then she stops and takes a step back as she stares at me. "What happened to your hair? And where did you get those clothes?"

"I got them from a dry cleaner's," I say. "It's no big deal. I'm going to put them back."

"Yeah, right," she says angrily. "That's how it starts. No big deal and I promise I'll put it right."

I shake my head. "It's not like that," I insist. "Dad asked for a few days. I need to find out what's going on."

"It's obvious what's going on! Your dad nicked a load of diamonds—" she starts, but I interrupt her.

"Look, Bunny," I said. "I know what you think but I've worked something out."

She rolls her eyes.

"My dad said he couldn't trust the police, which means the only person in the world that's on his side is me. Unless I do something he's in big trouble so I have to try."

Bunny leans closer; her eyes are wide and she looks so angry I am shocked. "Even if you don't like what you find?" she says.

"Even if I don't like what I find," I say. "So don't try and stop me."

Bunny folds her arms. "I'm not going to stop you," she says quietly. "You need to stop yourself. Sometimes parents aren't what you want them to be." She holds my eyes for a moment. "You have to make good decisions now, Archie," she says. "Before it's too late and you wreck your life. Take it from me because I know."

I know what she is saying. "I'm not going to break the law."

She crosses her arms. "I don't know every law there is, but I rather think stealing those clothes was a crime."

"You know what I mean," I say aggressively. And then I hesitate. "I just want to help him."

For a moment I think she is going to laugh. Then she shakes her head and sighs heavily.

"Don't get me wrong," she says. "You look different, but this is a life you don't know about. Don't expect me to help you."

"I don't want your help. I'm better off on my own."

Bunny snorts. "Good," she says. "Because if your

dad ends up in jail, that's how you'll be most of the time."

There's something sad about the way she says it, but before I can say anything the hard shell is back. "Anyway," she says. "Time's up. You need to go."

"I need another hour," I say. "I've got one more name to find."

I am still holding Dad's list, but she grabs it from my fingers and stares at it. "What are they?"

"Owners of precious stones."

I see her scanning the names until suddenly she frowns. She looks up at me. "All of them?"

"I don't know about Radcliffe's."

I can tell from her expression that it means something to her but she's not sure whether to tell me. She holds out the page but doesn't let go for a moment.

"It's a jewellery shop in Brighton," she says. "Radcliffe must be the bloke who owns it."

I stare at her. "How do you know?"

Bunny lets go of the page and walks over to get a glass of water at the sink. "Dad was watching it," she says slowly. "Two days before he got pulled. I bumped into him, sitting in town just staring at the place and when I asked him what he was doing he lied about it. Said he was thinking of buying a gift." She looks back at me. "If Tony Taylor wants jewellery, he doesn't buy it from a shop."

It seems more than a coincidence and I sense that Bunny thinks so too. She looks thoughtful while she drinks her water. Then she puts the glass down and turns back to me.

"So you don't need an hour, do you? Time to go."

I ignore her. "I need to go and look at that shop," I say.

She shakes her head as she marches towards the door. "Great," she says. "Buy me something nice. And don't ever give it to me."

She waits with her hand on the door handle but I'm not ready to leave. I need to work out what to do.

"Wait," I urge again. And then I have an idea. "You can't throw me out now. You said yourself the place is crawling with police. If I wait until it's dark, I won't get caught. Otherwise I might lead them back to this place."

She stares at me with wide eyes and an outraged expression. "You wouldn't dare," she hisses, but I don't have any other tricks to pull.

"Just give me until nightfall," I say. "Then no one will see me."

She stares at me and I guess she must realise she doesn't have much choice. Her face is set in frustration and she relents. "Fine," she says. "You've got until tonight. But I want the keys back now. You let yourself out and get lost, all right?"

I'm so relieved I almost smile, but I don't. I just nod and throw the keys down on the table. Bunny picks them up.

Then she marches over to me and pokes her finger into my chest. "You've never heard of this place, right? You've never been near it and if anyone asks, you've never heard of Tony Taylor, got that? If I ever see you again, you'll regret it."

"Suits me," I say.

"Suits me too."

She waits for a moment, just staring at me until she thinks she's made her point. Then she leaves, slamming the door behind her. I don't care. I'll go to that jeweller's and if I don't find answers there, I haven't lost anything because I've got nothing else to lose, have I?

And now I've got nowhere else to go.

WEDNESDAY
12.31 a.m.

Radcliffe's Jewellers, Gold and Silver Smiths, is a crooked three-storey building down a narrow lane in the middle of Brighton. It backs on to a small square filled with tables and chairs from a café that does Spanish food in the evening but is now dark and deserted. Two cameras point out above the square, fixed in position over the seating area, but I'm dressed in black and the back of the building is clear if I stay hidden in the shadows next to the wall.

The jewellery shop is on the ground floor. Over the first and second floors is an apartment where I guess Radcliffe lives. My heart is pounding but there's no one around. It's now or never. Staying silent, I slide along until I reach the steps that rise up to the back door of the apartment.

The rear door leads to a kitchen and I'm relieved I can't see the red light of a motion sensor inside. I guess the security system for the shop will be pretty sophisticated but I'm not there yet. And there's nothing valuable in the kitchen.

The kitchen door is wood at the bottom with glass panels and I can tell the keys have been left in the lock so I dig through all the stuff I've brought from the house and take out a large rubber plug along with a pair of diamond-tipped glass cutters shaped like a pair of compasses. I stick the plug on to one of the glass panels, then twist the lever at the back to hold it in place before scoring along the edge of the glass pane with the cutters, each stroke no more than a cough in the night. Then I remove the pane of glass still attached to the plug and reach inside to open the door. Once I am in, I fit the pane back into place with fast-acting superglue, holding it to dry for a minute, trying to stay silent while fear and exhilaration seem to rage inside me. I take my fingers away, waiting anxiously in case the glue fails, but it holds. Finally I can look around.

The kitchen is tidy with wooden cupboards and dark work surfaces. There is a fridge in the corner and a mug rack on one side next to a kettle and teapot. Next to the sink there is a small pile of newspapers, torn-up junk mail, a bottle and an empty Coke can ready to be recycled. Otherwise, the surfaces are clear.

Two doors lead out of the kitchen. One goes into the living room at the front of the building, the other one opens to my left on to a small landing from which a staircase goes up and down. I go down to the ground floor, where the stairs twist around to the right, and I am facing a large closed door. To my right a short passage leads to the wall of the back of the house, ending in the barred window I saw from outside.

There is a cupboard under the stairs that doesn't contain much except a few bright-red "sale" signs, a box of decorations from an old event and a whole bunch of spiders that scatter in all directions as my torch beam waves over them. Then I turn back to the large door. It's a purpose-built, steel-framed security door, protected by titanium-plated hinges. Behind it will be the strongroom where the stock is stored at night and probably the office where Radcliffe keeps his files. There will be a matching door on the other side, leading into the shop. The room is completely secure.

I sit on the foot of the stairs and stare at the solid door in front of me, feeling every second as it ticks by, knowing I don't have much time. To the left of the door frame is a keypad for a pretty standard motion-activated alarm system. It is good quality and reliable. And difficult to get past.

What have you got, what haven't you got and what are your options? Dad used to say, and I'm looking at the door trying to work it out. I can't smash through it and even if I could that would be noisy so I rule it out. I could try and find a way through the alarm system but there are numbers and letters so there's no way I can guess the code. I wonder if I should have spent some more time trying to understand some of the hacking kit in the house but I needed to get moving. I rub my face in my hands. *Think*, I urge myself. *Think!*

I have an idea. I run my fingers along the bottom of the door and find a slight gap between it and the carpet. Then I go back to the cupboard and spend a minute rummaging through the decorations until I find a balloon, then carefully gather as many spiders as I can get safely into my jacket pocket. Finally I creep back upstairs and turn on the tap a fraction. The pipes groan and I feel my heart speeding up but they settle quickly until the water trickles out silently. I let the water run, timing its flow on my phone before placing a bottle carefully on top of a

Coke can and sliding it under the dribbling tap so it starts to fill.

Then I hurry downstairs again, lie flat on my stomach in front of the door and push the balloon through the small gap. After five large puffs to inflate it on the other side of the door, I let go and it rushes violently out of my fingers, under the door and into the room.

Within a second, a high-pitched wailing alarm screams out from a speaker above me, loud enough to wake most of the street. A door slams somewhere upstairs. Lights go on and I can hear the heavy tramp of footsteps. I jump up and duck into the cupboard under the stairs, pulling the door almost shut behind me.

"What is it, Dad?" a boy's voice calls from upstairs.

"I don't know." The reply is muffled then clear as a man who must be Radcliffe opens the landing door and begins to come down. "Go back to bed."

But I can hear two sets of footsteps thumping on the stairs. The boy speaks again. "I can't sleep in this. Why's it gone off?"

Then Radcliffe is outside the cupboard, examining the screen above the keypad. He is wearing a dark-blue dressing gown with bare feet under his pyjama trousers.

"Sensor two, inside the strongroom, has gone off," he says loudly over the sound of the siren. "Although sensor one in the shop hasn't gone off and there's no sign of disturbance from here."

There are more steps on the stairs above me, then I can see the boy. He is ten or eleven and skinny, in a T-shirt and pyjama shorts with freckles on his neck and arms.

"Shall I call the police?" he shouts.

"NO!" Radcliffe yells, suddenly turning to face him on the stairs. "No, no need for that. I'll just have a quick look and check everything's all right." Radcliffe is speaking more calmly now, but I can tell he wouldn't be happy if the police turned up.

He taps six buttons on the keypad and at last the wailing stops. Then he pushes four more buttons and there is a *clunk* as the door unlocks itself and swings open. I stretch to see, but Radcliffe is in the way and I can't read the code.

The boy leans on the door, looking into the room. "I thought we had to call the police if the alarm went off? For the insurance."

"Let's just check if it's anything first," says Radcliffe, and he steps into the room. I push the cupboard door slightly further open and listen as he looks around the strongroom.

"That's weird," he says. "Nothing's been moved. Both the doors were shut properly—"

There is a crash from upstairs and he stops abruptly. The bottle I put under the tap has filled and fallen off the can it was balanced on so both have tumbled into the sink.

Radcliffe bursts out of the strongroom. "What was that?" he says. "There's someone upstairs!"

He rushes upstairs with the boy behind him. I slip out of the cupboard and into the strongroom. I've got about fifteen seconds before they come back and I look around but the only furniture in the room consists of three locked jewellery cabinets, a long plain work table, a small sink and a small chest of drawers.

I stare around frantically, but that's all there is. There's nowhere to hide.

WEDNESDAY
2.37 a.m.

I can hear the Radcliffes' voices as they come down the stairs and there is no other option. I slide under the table, bracing my arms and legs against the large lip and forcing myself to hang underneath it like a starfish. My muscles start to burn almost immediately as they take my weight and I curse myself for not thinking of something better. I've got no idea how long I can hang here but I am about to find out.

"One of us must have left the recycling piled in the sink with the tap dripping," Radcliffe is saying, "and I don't think it was me!"

"I don't see why I get blamed for everything," the kid says. "You probably think the alarm going off was my fault too."

"I don't know what that was." Radcliffe pauses. "Hold on. There's a damn spider on that sensor; I bet that's what it was. Those little devils get everywhere."

Sweat is running down into my eyes and I watch Radcliffe's bare feet move to the corner of the room. I close them and focus on my arms, which are screaming in pain. I can't hold on much longer.

"There's another one!" Radcliffe exclaims, and I feel a swoosh of movement above me as Radcliffe hits out at something, but it seems half-hearted. He sighs. "We'll have to turn the alarm off tonight and give the room a good clean tomorrow."

My plan seems to have fooled them, but now I'm desperate for them to leave. My breath is coming in gasps and each one is getting louder. The pain has spread from my arms through my shoulders and into my back. My thighs and calves are aching where I am pushing as hard as I can into the table and every part of my body wants to let go, but I force myself on. In my mind I picture my mum, sitting with me at the hospital when I broke my wrist, telling me to be strong, telling me to be brave, and I open my eyes again.

The carpet tiles are a kind of green, I think, and I clench my teeth and focus on my breathing. There is yellow on the bottom of Radcliffe's dressing gown...

"We'll leave it for the morning," Radcliffe says. "It's

too late now," and he switches off the light but the door is still open.

The table is brown. Radcliffe is still speaking, saying something about going on holiday. I hear myself gasp but I can't stop it. I'm desperately looking around for something blue. I can hold on if I find something but I can't see anything. Blood is pounding in my head and I am going to collapse.

"How about America?" the kid says. "Why don't we go on holiday there?"

"Sure," Radcliffe says as he pulls the heavy door shut. "There's no point earning it if you don't spend it, is there?"

The room is plunged into darkness and I crash to the floor. Somehow I have done it, but every fibre of my body is in agony. I lie back, breathing hard, and stare up at the little blue manufacturer's sticker on the underside of the table that had been in front of me the whole time. That was too close, I think. Much too close.

I lie panting for a few minutes until my legs stop burning and my breath returns to normal. Then I sit up and grab the lamp from my bag, turning it on and illuminating the enclosed room with a white, ghostly light. I look up at the sensor that I pulled out from the wall and then at the time. It is two forty and I want to be out before it gets light. That gives me about two hours.

I open the stock cabinets and check inside but there is nothing very expensive and that's not why I'm here. Next to the sink there's a strange machine that looks like an old-fashioned record turntable with prongs sticking out of it, and beside that is a unit of drawers full of specialist magnifying glasses. On a shelf is a set of chemical bottles labelled *boric acid*, *refined alcohol*, *distilled water* and *clear oil* but I have no idea what any of this stuff is for. I take some pictures of it on my phone anyway. Because I don't quite know what else to do.

I guess I didn't expect to find some big clue that would tell me what was going on and how my dad was involved, but I thought there might be something to explain why Radcliffe's name was on that list. The files on the shelves are bulging with papers but as I go through them there is nothing that looks suspicious. Just pages and pages that seem to show what Radcliffe has bought and sold, and a whole load of bills that go back years. As I flick through a file stuffed with hundreds of bank statements, each filled with thousands of seemingly irrelevant transactions, I'm beginning to think this is all just a waste of time.

There is nothing else to see so I get up and try to close the file. Except one of the pages has jammed in the lever arch. I open it again on the desk and take out the page to unjam it, then hesitate when I see it is different. It's a Radcliffe's Jewellers bank statement but it's with the First International Bank of Israel instead of Radcliffe's normal bank. And there are no transactions listed on it.

I wonder why a small Brighton jeweller would need an Israeli bank account that he doesn't seem to use and I flick through the file again until I find a pattern. For every twenty pages of standard statements, there's a single page for the Israeli account. But none of these have any transactions listed and that doesn't make sense. If there are no transactions, why hold the account?

I have to go through almost every page before finally I find something. It's dated eight months ago and there are two entries. The first is a deposit for four hundred and forty thousand dollars from someone called Xavier Carmichael. The second is a payment for four hundred thousand dollars to an account that is just a number. I'm not the best at maths, but even I can see that the payment received is exactly ten percent more than the money out. But there's no other detail about who the money ends up going to.

I stare at the page, feeling like I'm on to something but I don't know what, and when the alarm on my phone buzzes I know I have to get out. I put the pages back in the file and check around the room to make sure that nothing is disturbed. Then I hesitate by the door.

This payment is so much bigger than all the others and so out of the ordinary that it seems suspicious. I wonder how much the Madagascan diamond necklace is worth and the more I think about it, the more I am sure this is the sort of payment that might be made for something that valuable. Except, why is the money in that account going to Israel?

This payment feels wrong and if Radcliffe's name was on Dad's list I reckon it must be to do with the jewellery thefts, but I don't know why. I need to find out about Carmichael but I can't do that if I'm captured by the police or sleeping rough somewhere.

I try and think of my options but there is only one I can see.

Bunny took the keys, but we both know that doors can be unlocked without them. I don't know how mad she'll be if I go back but I'm not sure I have a choice. Maybe I'll regret it but I'm too tired to go anywhere else. I'll go to the house, get some sleep and be gone before she checks. *Decision made*, I think. It's time to go.

The security door can be opened with a lever from the inside to stop people getting trapped by accident, but the solid *clunk* is louder than I expect and it jolts me out of my thoughts. I dart out of the room and sprint up the stairs just as a light flicks on, sending shadows into the stairwell. I haven't got time to be cautious and it doesn't matter now anyway so I just throw open the kitchen door, race out into the dawn, grabbing the green rental bike that I borrowed from a rack on the seafront and tearing back as fast as I can.

When I get to Stevenson Close, I jump over the garden gate and run around to the back door, then pick the lock carefully and go in, feeling the relief wash through me.

But before I can take two steps I hear a loud pop

and some kind of net explodes then wraps around my body. I try to wrestle free but it seems to be sticky and the more I move, the more wrapped up I become. Within a few seconds I am lying on the floor like the filling in a spring roll. My arms are trapped by my sides and the only part of me that can move is my toes. I can't shout for help and I can't escape. The house seems to be deserted and I am alone.

So I do the only thing I can. I go to sleep.

WEDNESDAY
11.25 a.m.

"The idiot returns. Did you really think I was stupid enough to trust you?"

It is Bunny's voice. When I open my eyes I can just see her feet where she is sitting on one of the kitchen chairs. Clean white Adidas trainers below bare ankles. I rock on to my side, which causes every muscle in my body to scream in agony, but at least now I can see her face. I expect her to look furious but she seems to find it funny.

"Are you going to let me out of this?"

"Clever, isn't it?" she says. "I found it in the attic room. It's like Velcro, only stronger, and the more you move the more it sticks to itself. You can peel it off easily but not when you're in it." Her voice hardens. "Are you going to answer my question?"

"I couldn't go anywhere else."

"You couldn't come here!"

I don't reply.

"You left the house at half past eleven and set off my anti-idiot device at four oh eight so I assume you had some fun in between. Did you find anything at the jeweller?"

My neck hurts as I try and look at her so I roll on to my back and stare at the ceiling. "Something," I say. "But I don't know what. There are pictures on my phone."

"My dad's phone, you mean."

Before I can answer, she strides over to me and checks my pockets to locate the phone. Then I hear a kind of ripping sound as she loosens the net and takes the phone before tightening the binds again.

But when she starts to look at the pictures, her tone changes. "Wow," she says. "You have been busy. I wonder what he's up to."

"Are you going to let me out?"

"Do you know what this stuff is?" she asks thoughtfully.

"I'd shake my head, but I can't. At least let me sit up. I'm getting cramp."

She looks away from the phone for a moment, prodding me with her foot. "You promise not to run away?"

126

"I promise," I say exasperatedly. "Please, Bunny. Let me out!"

As she struggles to keep the smirk off her face, she kneels down next to me and unwraps the net from my feet. When my legs are free I stretch them out and sit up, at last feeling the blood flow through me. She doesn't release my arms, but moves away to put the kettle on, taking two mugs from a cupboard and putting a tea bag in each.

"Are you going to be good?" she asks.

"I'm sorry," I say. "I didn't know what else to do."

She comes back across and starts to undo the rest of the net.

"Your dad's mixed up in this too," I say. "Why else would he have been watching Radcliffe's or given my dad the keys to this place?"

"I know," she says. "I've been thinking about that all night. But my dad's a crook, no matter what he said—" She stops abruptly, thinking for a moment, before grimacing and releasing my hands so I can free myself. Then she walks back over to the kettle and makes the tea.

"What did he say?" I ask.

She shrugs. "Before they took him away, he said

something had changed and he was going to make things right. He promised he was going to go legit."

She throws the spoon angrily into the sink. "I believed him too. Even the judge seemed to believe him. She dismissed most of the charges and would have given him bail if his track record wasn't so bad. Dad seemed relaxed, like things were changing." She turns and stares at me. "So why's he kept all that stuff in the loft?"

"You can't just dump that sort of stuff," I say. "Maybe he didn't have a chance to get rid of it."

She pulls a face. "He's a middleman," she says. "He gets criminals anything they want to get, and gets rid of anything they want to get rid of. And his speciality is precious stones. Your dad gets caught stealing a load of diamonds..." She shakes her head. "That means my dad's in this up to his neck. The only thing he's better at than helping criminals is breaking promises."

I stare at her as the sunlight slants across her face.

"Look," I say. "They were into something together, which either means they're both guilty or they're both innocent. I'm prepared to take a risk for my dad. Won't you take a risk for yours? You could help me.

Tell me some of the things you know and let me stay here. Just for a day or two. We won't break the law, trust me."

But she shakes her head and speaks in an angry tone. "You can't trust anyone, Archie. First rule, right?"

"But what if he was telling the truth? Would you forgive yourself if you didn't help him?"

Her eyes flash and she starts to speak before stopping herself and I wonder if I've hit a nerve. Then she looks away and seems to think for a long time, staring out of the window before turning back to me and shrugging.

"I don't know," she admits.

She turns away again, before tipping her head back and groaning, louder than I expect, as if the frustration is pouring out of her. Until eventually the groan turns into a kind of laugh and she shakes her head again.

"You're not going to give up, are you?"

"No."

She drums her fingers on the worktop. "And you're way too much of an idiot to be allowed to run around on your own, aren't you?"

"Way too much," I agree.

"Way, way too much," she repeats, picking up the tea and bringing it over, banging the mugs in front of me on the table, although I get the impression the anger has gone.

"Fine," she says, and for the first time in ages I feel like something's gone my way. I grin and eventually she grins back. She rolls her eyes and tells me again that I'm an idiot, but funnily I feel like it's the nicest thing anyone's said to me in ages.

"Fine," she repeats. "But we stop when I say. And if you get caught you're on your own."

I nod. Then I realise I'm still grinning, so I force myself to stop and be serious again. I think back to what I saw last night. "So what do the pictures on the phone mean?" I ask. "You seemed to know what that stuff was for."

"I do," Bunny says. "Dad looked after kit like that for a mate once. That machine and those chemicals are for cutting precious stones."

"How do you cut stones? I thought diamonds were supposed to be harder than anything."

Bunny shakes her head. "Diamonds don't come out of the ground like you see them in the shops," she says. "Most precious stones are rough and dirty

130

before they're cut." She smiles. "My dad would always joke they were just like him."

Now it's my turn to roll my eyes. "Go on."

"They're just shapeless lumps of coloured rock," she says. "Cutting them shaves off the outer dirty surface and turns them into the final design that you see. Mostly it's about getting the largest clean stone you can from the original lump."

"What do you mean, clean?"

"Perfect, no flaws," she says. "And you've got to be pretty talented to cut stones because a good cut can mean a massive difference in value to a diamond or any other stone."

"So have most jewellers got this equipment in their shops?"

"No way," she says. "It's expensive and difficult to use. Most jewellers will buy stuff ready to sell from wholesalers, and most stones are cut overseas."

"What about the money?" I say. "Radcliffe's got this Israeli bank account with only two transactions. Someone called Carmichael sent him a load of money then he paid most of it to someone else straight away."

Bunny frowns. "Sounds like Carmichael was paying

for something that Radcliffe bought for him."

"The stolen diamonds?"

Bunny shrugs. "Could be. But I don't know what Israel's got to do with it. I'll call one of Dad's mates now. See if they've got any idea."

She takes out her phone and goes into the garden for a minute. And when she gets back I'm almost bursting to tell her what I've found online.

"Xavier Carmichael's a local auctioneer," I say. "Looks like he's quite famous. There's a charity auction this afternoon at the Grand Hotel."

"We should go," she says quickly, and then she holds up her hands before I can speak. "And I only said 'we' because if I leave you on your own you'll get caught before we've found out anything useful. I want to know what's going on." She sighs. "Maybe Dad wasn't lying. And if he wasn't I want to know."

She looks at her watch. "What time is the auction?"

"Two o'clock."

"That's fine," she says. "But I've got to pick up Little Tony from nursery at four. I can't be late."

"Who's Little Tony?"

"He's my brother," she says, and there is a look in her eye as if it is a challenge. "And he's more important

132

than any of this, all right?"

I'm surprised at how aggressively she says it and I wonder if I should have been as determined to keep her out of things, but I guess it's too late now. I glance at my phone and it's already past midday.

I need to get changed and I hurry towards the stairs before suddenly I hesitate. "Thanks, Bunny," I say. "This means a lot to me."

"Idiot," she says again.

But finally I feel like someone's on my side.

WEDNESDAY
1.04 p.m.

I had forgotten about the police. I guess in the dark of last night I didn't give them much thought. But as soon as we sit at the bus stop to wait, Bunny stops talking and I know something's wrong. I was looking at my phone trying to find more about Carmichael but when I glance up, two community support officers are walking their bikes down the road towards us. Panic floods my body and I tense myself to run, except when I do Bunny's hand clamps down on my arm.

"Keep still," she hisses. "If you run, they'll notice and follow."

She is right. I twist away slightly so that she's between me and them, then I pull the black-framed glasses out of my bag and put them on, watching through the clear lenses as they walk slowly up the street.

They look pretty relaxed and they might not be here

for me, but I've got a horrible feeling that they are. Behind them a bus turns away from the sea towards us. "OK, Archie," Bunny murmurs. "We're going to sit nice and still and then we're going to get on the bus. You look different, so stay calm, all right?"

"All right," I say, although I don't feel it. The bus's brakes groan and it slows and stops. The doors hiss open and we get on before the officers reach us. I'm doing whatever I can in my head to focus, except I can't look around to see any colours because I have to keep my head facing forward. I force myself to try and act normal but it is hard. Bunny scans her pass through the machine and I ask for a day saver ticket, keeping my back to the open door. Before the driver can respond he is interrupted.

One of the police officers has stepped on to the bus and is standing behind me. I look away but there is nowhere I can go as he is blocking the door. I shuffle along, stare at the floor and wait.

The policeman hands the driver a photocopied piece of paper. "We're looking for this kid. Have you seen him?"

My heart is pounding like it's going to explode because I just know it's a picture of me. "We'd like you to keep an eye out for him," the officer says. "If you see him, or think you see him, let us know right away. And, if you can, keep him on the bus."

The driver holds it up and, as I glance across, I try not to react. It's a selfie we took on Dad's phone about a year ago, in front of an open strongbox, the second time I ever won a race. I can see myself with Dad's arm around me and I'm laughing. I remember how Dad had spent about half an hour getting the lock open and he'd thought he'd set a really good time so he was bound to win. Except I just smashed off the hinges in a minute. I can see his face in my mind, grumpy and saying it wasn't right to smash something that had been designed so carefully, but he could only hold that look for a minute and after that he just laughed and admitted he didn't think about it and then we took the photo.

I don't know how they got it as we never printed it out, because Mum did all that sort of stuff. Me and Dad never quite thought about it like she did.

Bunny is gripping my arm tight, forcing me back to the present. She pushes me forward as the driver tucks the photo away next to his window and at last the policeman gets off. The driver turns back to me and now I can sense him staring. Bunny waved her phone at the scanner and I am trying to look anywhere but at him. I look for something green on the bus and settle on a woman's T-shirt. I search for something yellow.

"Hold on a minute," the driver says. "You!"

I turn and he is pointing at me. The policeman has got off but we are not moving yet and they are only metres away.

"Is there a problem?" Bunny asks, but the driver ignores her. I raise my eyes to meet his.

"Me?" I ask.

He nods. "You've got to be fourteen for that ticket. And if you're only fourteen, I'm a hundred. So unless you've got some ID you pay the full fare or you get off my bus."

I almost take my wallet out of my pocket and show my school card, then remember not to. "I'm sorry," I say. "I thought it was sixteen. I don't mind paying."

He shakes his head as if I was trying to cheat him. We pay the extra and race upstairs, slumping into seats near the front where I watch the police officers walking up the street.

"Calm as a hand grenade," Bunny grunts, but I'm

too stressed to react. I remind myself that every step I take forward I'm helping Dad. But I don't know if that's true. And I don't know how much longer I can keep this up.

WEDNESDAY
1.41 p.m.

The bus arrives in the centre of Brighton and we get off, walking along the seafront away from the noise and lights and wild rides of the old wooden pier. Everywhere is packed with people enjoying the holiday sunshine but even in the crowd I keep my head down, feeling as if every pair of eyes is on me.

Bunny seems to sense this and leads the way quickly, weaving through the people with her phone clamped to her ear until we are opposite the huge eight-storey Grand Hotel, which sits proudly facing out to sea, its rows of windows sparkling like diamonds in the sunshine. The revolving door at the front is manned by a uniformed porter, but he seems mostly engaged with getting taxis and doesn't pay much attention to the stream of people coming in and out.

I pull my cap down hard and am about to march

across the road when Bunny cuts the latest call and stops me.

Her face is dark. "We need to talk first," she says, dragging me towards an empty bench that overlooks the stony beach. "It turns out Israel is where you buy precious stones. New ones from the African mines. Before they've been cut."

I look across at her. "So what?" I say. "Dad's list of names were all people who were robbed. Radcliffe must have planned to use that kit to cut the stolen stones so he can sell them through his shop. Maybe Dad thought Radcliffe could lead him to the thieves."

Then another thought strikes me and my heart sinks. What if Dad had Radcliffe's name because he was going to sell Radcliffe the necklace? I stare at Bunny anxiously, wondering if she's thinking the same, but she shakes her head.

"There's no point stealing massive diamonds if you're going to cut them up," she says. "Big stones are seriously rare. They're worth stacks more if they're whole. The payments to Israel must be for new stones that they're cutting here. But I don't know why."

"Something doesn't add up," I say. "But we need to

go or we'll miss the auction."

Before I can move, though, Bunny grabs my arm. "I've heard something else," she says. "They've moved your dad to Lewes."

I can feel my body tense. "What does that mean?"

There is fear in her eyes that sends a chill through me. "Lewes is a proper prison," she says. "They don't want him in a police station any more."

Suddenly I feel a wave of fear rush through me because I know that's bad. Police officers aren't safe in prisons – not surrounded by the criminals they've put there.

"How do you know?" I ask.

She hesitates and I can tell she is holding something back, but then she says, "I got a message from my dad. He's in Lewes too."

"I thought you weren't allowed phones in prison," I say, but she shrugs.

"There's loads of ways to get them through security scanners, but he can't talk openly and only leaves messages." She looks awkward or guilty or something. "You can listen if you like, but it's not good."

I hardly want to take the phone even though I've

been desperate for news. I lift it to my ear as the gruff voice starts speaking.

"Hi, Treacle. I got your message and you might be right. I keep hearing there's a group targeting historical pieces but I don't know more than that. Blake's hearing is on Friday and they've moved him here until then.

"Everyone thinks he took those diamonds and now the sharks are circling and he's out of his depth. If you find yourself anywhere near that necklace, you walk away as fast as you can, OK? No one I know will hurt you but they don't care about Blake and they don't care about that kid. So if it comes to it, you just walk away."

I can tell from his voice he is getting worked up. Then he breaks off and when he speaks again his voice is kind of sad and resigned.

"The whole thing's a mess, baby. It's the world I'm in. It gets you a little bit more each day until your soul is sick and you can't see a way out. I thought me and Blake could..."

The gruff voice hesitates and I can imagine him trying to find the right words.

"I thought I found one, but maybe all I've done is

spread the sickness a little further. You're a diamond, baby, so keep sparkling and stay safe," he says finally. *"I love you and I'll see you soon."*

I hand the phone back to Bunny and stand up. "Well, we know they're working together now, don't we?" I ask.

She looks down at the ground, avoiding my eyes. "Let's just keep going." She looks up at me and tries to smile. "If we can work out what's going on..."

The roar of an engine interrupts her and I look up as a black Aston Martin with the number plate XC007 pulls up in front of the hotel too quickly, scattering the group of tourists outside it. A large man in his forties, who I recognise from my Internet search as Xavier Carmichael, gets out and marches up to the porter. He has fleshy features and short dark curly hair that he has tried unsuccessfully to smooth down and he's dressed in what looks like an expensive blue suit. He moves impatiently, with his car key in one hand and a bulging leather briefcase in the other.

As we hurry across the road, I hear him bark at the porter. "I'm doing a charity auction, for God's sake. The least you can do is park my damn car." Then he practically throws the key at him and marches into the hotel.

We follow, while the porter is busy with the car, entering the wide, marble-floored reception area where a large sign advertises Hailsham Trust Auction, which is taking place in the Napoleon room on the second floor. Carmichael is talking to a member of staff who seems relieved that he has turned up at last and is offering to carry Carmichael's briefcase in an attempt to get him to hurry. But as he reaches for it, Carmichael pulls it sharply away.

"No!" he snaps loudly, causing several heads to turn. "Don't you dare touch this bag. Now, let's just get this done."

As they head towards the lifts, Bunny nods towards the wide, sweeping staircase in front of us and I follow her.

"Now what?" she asks.

I shrug. "He's pretty protective about that briefcase," I whisper. "Maybe we should take a look at it."

"How the hell are you going to do that?"

"I don't know," I start, and then I stop. After two flights, the stairs open into a wide landing where around fifty wealthy-looking people are mingling, talking loudly, while several assistants with clipboards circulate, ticking names off a list and handing out red paddles that look like small table tennis bats with numbers written on them.

Behind them, a rope barrier cordons off double doors that open on to a room that has clearly been laid out for the auction, with chairs arranged in two blocks in front of a long table.

On one side of the table is an empty pedestal; on the other is a single chair. A small wooden auctioneer's hammer rests next to a bottle of mineral water and a glass, set on a thick white Grand Hotel-stamped tablecloth.

At the top of the stairs and on either side of the roped-off doorway stand blue-uniformed security guards.

"They're not looking for you," whispers Bunny. "They're here to guard whatever's being sold," and I know she's right, but as we continue up to the busy space I feel more and more out of place. Everyone here is an adult and looks rich enough to spend a fortune. I'm wearing a suit, but Bunny is in jeans and we're definitely not on whatever list the assistants are checking names off.

From the corner of my eye I see a guard stare at us then gesture to a member of the hotel staff and I realise we've got seconds before we're asked to leave. I pull Bunny towards a window recess where we turn our backs to the room, facing a small balcony and the sea beyond.

"I need a diversion," I hiss. "Now."

Bunny stares at me for a fraction of a second, then she winks and all hell seems to break loose.

WEDNESDAY
1.56 p.m.

Bunny's voice rips across the background chatter. "Dad!" she yells. "Dad!"

From the corner of my eye I see the security guard stiffen, then follow the assistant urgently towards Bunny, who is moving away into the middle of the busy landing. She is waving her phone in the air, shouting out something about her dad leaving his phone behind and needing it for the auction. Everyone turns towards her and all conversation seems to stop.

Meanwhile I step out on to the balcony, climb up on to the metal grille on my right and jump across the short gap to the next balcony along.

I don't know if anyone on the street below has noticed and I don't have time to care. My heart pounding, I spring up and dart inside the empty auction room, then run forward and duck under the tablecloth that covers the table at the front. Outside, I hear the commotion dying down then a firm voice telling Bunny that her father isn't here and it's time she left. In the gloomy space below the table I wait, while the general buzz and chatter starts back up then gets louder as guests are allowed in. The room goes silent again and I wonder what is going on, until there is a thump on the other side of the cloth as Carmichael's briefcase is dropped to the floor and his feet shoot under the table next to me.

I scramble out of the way, grateful for the thick carpet that covers any sound, then settle and listen as he introduces the auction in smooth, cheerful tones that seem completely false after the way he spoke to the porter. He makes a joke, warning the gathering not to sneeze in case he thinks it's a bid, and the room laughs happily. Then he starts the auction.

I can't see what's being sold but some of the prices seem astonishing. There are twenty items to be auctioned in increasing order of value and Carmichael repeatedly reminds everyone that the auction is for charity so they should be generous. He has valued the pieces himself, he adds, and he won't take anything less than they're worth. The first item is described as a nineteenth-century painting of some spaniels, which sells for thirty-five thousand pounds, followed by a pair of gold cufflinks that had been worn by an officer on the *Titanic* and sells for forty thousand. As the bidding starts on the third lot, I notice how Carmichael is restless between items, but once the bidding starts he sits very still. When he next bangs the wooden hammer down to indicate the end of the bidding for a fourth time, I roll over and stretch out so I am lying flat, then wait for Carmichael to start things off again. When he does, I raise the tablecloth a fraction so I can see the bottom of the briefcase. Then I reach out and slide it a few centimetres towards me.

Carmichael doesn't notice. He doesn't notice as I pull it further. And then further, until it is practically under the table but still on his side of the cloth. Then, with my heart in my mouth, I wait for the hammer to come down one more time.

And whip the tablecloth up and over the case.

Nothing happens. I'm half expecting him to jump up in shock and I'm ready to run if he does, but he simply rearranges himself, stretching out his legs before introducing another item. I glance at my watch; I've got maybe another half an hour even if he doesn't notice the case has been moved. I hold my fingers over the two spring-loaded catches that lock the case and try to open it. They don't move.

It's frustrating but it shouldn't take me long to open. Quickly, I untie one of my shoes, pull the lace out and tie it in a loop around one of the table legs. Then I move the case so the other side of the loop is around the button to open the first lock, pulling it tight to create a constant pressure. Now I race through the numbers with both hands, spinning the dial on the right and turning the other two dials until, after two minutes, I get to four-three-three and the catch springs open. Turning the case around, I wrap the lace around the second button and turn the next set of dials. And within another three minutes, the case is open.

It's hard to see much in the dark so I turn my phone torch on, then start emptying the case. I am shocked to see that most of what's inside is old newspapers and I wonder if it's some weird attempt by Carmichael to make himself look important. I ignore them but there is not much left, just a diary and a card folder with letters and emails in it.

I flick through the correspondence, most of which seems to be letters telling Carmichael that they don't want his services as a valuer. Some of them are from grand-sounding households and one is from the secretary to a duke. And when I look at the diary, I notice that among the entries for auctions and meetings and events, there are several that simply give a smart-sounding address followed by a figure in pounds. Castleton House is followed by *£250k*; Brokenhill is followed by *£475k*; and Edgar Hall is followed by *£1m???* It all looks pretty suspicious, even if it doesn't specifically mention jewellery, so I take pictures. And send them across to Bunny.

After a minute, Bunny messages back with a narrow-eyed emoji then she tells me she can't wait much longer and I realise I haven't been paying attention to the auction. Above me, Carmichael announces the last item. I start putting things back in the case in the order I took them out, as Carmichael describes a set of silver cufflinks given by George the Third to Nelson before the Battle of the Nile. He asks for opening bids of one hundred thousand pounds. I am shocked by how much more valuable they are than the other cufflinks, especially as they are silver and the others were gold, but the bidders seem keen to pay and soon the price is at two hundred thousand.

It's money I can't dream of, so I ignore it and focus on getting the papers back in the case, pausing to hold my phone in my teeth while I spread them out flat. The light shines on a page from *Racing Post* where Carmichael has made notes against a load of horses that were racing. I check another one and it is another *Racing Post* from the day before, with the next paper from the day before that. I wonder how much Carmichael bets and whether he wins, but now the time is up. The hammer bangs down on the table and the room bursts into a round of applause. Carmichael's feet stretch out again and then he sits up straight.

He thanks the crowd for their bids and announces that they have raised almost half a million pounds for the Hailsham Trust. He tells them that he is delighted to be hosting the post-auction party at his house that evening and he hopes they have all bought their tickets because proceeds are also going to the charity. Then he thanks them again and I hear a wave of noise as the guests all begin talking at once.

And, before I can react, the tablecloth is hauled up roughly, as Carmichael reaches for his briefcase.

Our eyes meet, and for a moment neither of us

reacts. Then I move.

Carmichael yells something incoherent and makes a grab for me, but I jerk under the cloth and out from the other side of the table, turning to see the whole room full of people staring. There are security guards in each corner, two by the door and more standing either side of the silver cufflinks, which sit on a white cushion on the pedestal at the end of the table. A woman screams, but I don't stop moving. There is no way out of the door so I sprint for the window, batting away the hands that grab at me, leaping over the outstretched arms of a guard who dives at me, until I find myself out on the narrow balcony where I got in. But this time a guard appears on the neighbouring balcony, and I am trapped.

I am about eight metres up from the street and there is only one way out. Ignoring the danger, I scramble over the metal railing then lower myself until I can swing down on to the balcony underneath. Below me now is the sloping glass roof of a conservatory and I don't know if the glass will be strong enough to take my weight, but I have no choice.

As two guards burst on to the balcony above, I swing myself over the next railing, then tumble down the smooth glass, desperately clinging to the white guttering as I spill over the edge. Everyone inside the conservatory looks up suddenly and I feel my loose shoe drop from my foot, but I ignore it and tip my legs over the parking area, jumping on to the top of a black taxi, then down again into the street. There are shouts from above and the pedestrians stare, but they don't know what's happening and they don't stop me.

I grab my shoe and within moments I am away, sprinting through the crowds until I see the bus stop ahead of me where Bunny is waiting next to a bus that's just pulled in. We jump on and head upstairs.

"I assume Cinderella made it to the ball then," Bunny says.

But I am panting too hard to answer.

WEDNESDAY
3.48 p.m.

"He must be a big part of it," I whisper as I rethread my shoelace. "All the pieces stolen were famous antiques and it's his job to go to rich people's houses and value things for them. People trust him. And he seems to bet on every horse race there is."

Bunny nods. "I looked up a few from the pictures you sent. Most of his bets lost. Looks like he's got a pretty nasty habit. Maybe he can't live without another source of income."

The bus pulls up to our stop and we get off. "He's hosting a charity party tonight. If I knew where he lived, I could go to it," I say. "Have a proper look around."

Bunny looks at me for a moment before pulling out her phone and dialling a number.

"Who are you calling?" I mouth at her, but she shakes her head and turns away.

"It's Bunny," she says. "Tony's girl. Yeah, I know, but

can you get me an address from a plate? It's XC007. Yeah, I know. An Aston. No, it's nothing to do with my dad. I'll owe you, not him. Text it to me, will you?" Then she hangs up.

When she cuts the call, she must see the time on her phone because she suddenly speeds up.

"We need to hurry," she says, "or we'll be late for my brother."

She is practically running and I have to jog to keep up, but fortunately it's not too far away. Little Tykes Nursery is a brightly coloured single-storey building, its windows decorated with rainbows and stars. When we arrive, Bunny joins a small stream of parents who go inside. She emerges after a minute holding the hand of a small boy who looks about three or four with a grubby face and stocky frame squeezed into blue shorts and a red T-shirt with the word *Awesome* blazed across the front. As they come out Bunny says something and the boy seems to crease up, his eyes shining as he bursts into laughter. They come over to me and suddenly Bunny seems nervous.

"This is Little Tony," she says. "Although David calls him Anthony. I've got to look after him this afternoon."

"David's your mum's...?"

I don't need to finish because she nods. Then she looks back at Little Tony and grins and sticks out her tongue so he explodes into giggles again before launching into a story about something he has been doing that afternoon with plasticine.

Behind her, a woman leaves the nursery with another boy. She takes his hand and leads him away past us, catching my eye for a moment before turning and walking to her old blue Honda, where she opens the rear door. She sweeps the boy into her arms and kisses him as she clips him into his seat before getting into the car and driving away.

I watch, trying to remember holding my mum's hand; trying to feel the heat of her fingers in mine, but there is nothing. I know she did. I even remember thinking that she always held my hand tighter when Dad was on a big case or when he was worried about something, but I can't quite recall the feeling.

Suddenly I feel sadder than I have in years.

Bunny tells Little Tony I'm her friend Archie, then laughs as he pulls on her arm and tries to count the seagulls in the sky. Until her phone buzzes and she checks it, turning to me and half whispering above

Little Tony's head.

"The car's registered address is a place called Lakehurst Manor about ten miles outside town," she says. "That must be where Carmichael lives." She plays with the map on her phone and then whistles though her teeth. "Blimey. It's huge. More like an estate than a house."

She holds the phone up and I see a massive house with large grounds surrounded by countryside.

"Fine," I say. "A big house like that with lots of people around. It should be easy to get in."

"Won't he remember you after today?"

I shrug because it doesn't matter. Dad's hearing is the day after tomorrow and I need to figure out how Carmichael and Radcliffe and everything else fits together. I don't have time to delay.

"The person who sent you this message," I say. "Are they a police officer?"

Bunny shrugs. "Dad knows a few boys in blue who will help out for a couple of quid," she says, then she looks embarrassed. "I mean—" she starts, but I interrupt.

"How many corrupt policemen are there?" I ask quietly.

Bunny looks guilty. "Not so many," she says. "But once they take a bribe or do something else wrong, the gangs can blackmail them into more crime. And they can get stuck in that life forever."

"If someone wanted to frame my dad, could they get one of them to help?"

Bunny hesitates. "Maybe," she says. "Or..." She stops.

"Or he could be one of them?"

She looks away and I realise Little Tony is listening carefully. I shrug. "I still want to go to that party."

Bunny sighs then takes out her phone, stepping away a few paces to make a call, talking to someone called Bob in a way where I recognise the words but can't seem to follow what she is saying. Little Tony seems happy enough to hold my hand and chatter about things I don't know about or understand, until he appears to notice the tension and just stares at me with big, thoughtful eyes.

And then I notice the men.

They are standing with their backs to me in front of one of the houses on the corner of Wilkinson Avenue, and as soon as I see them my mind flashes back to the night Mum died and all the energy seems to drain from my body. The smaller one is slightly hidden by a hedge, but I recognise his thick neck and scruffy, lazy stance as he complains to the taller one, who is standing calmly with one hand in his pocket and the other holding his phone. The smaller man keeps whinging, then the taller man suddenly turns and I get a glimpse of his piercing-blue eyes and open face, spoiled by a long scar that winds across his forehead. I force myself to breathe, but I can't tear my eyes away from him as he scratches his chin then points back towards the main road. The smaller man is still shaking his head and scowling, until suddenly he kicks a stone from the garden path, which rattles into the wall next to us.

Startling Little Tony. And ripping my thoughts back to the present.

The boy's blond head snaps up and a look of fear fills his big eyes. Bunny sees it and moves quickly to his side, pulling him up into her arms.

"Oi, watch it!" Bunny yells, and the man snarls at her angrily.

"Watch it yourself," he spits.

But I don't let her reply. I just force my body to move, marching to the other side of her with my head down, before reaching out and grabbing her sleeve, waving my hand in a kind of apology and pulling her arm hard so all she can do is follow me.

Two kids and a small boy, walking home. I just pray he hasn't recognised me.

"We ain't got time to do this again," I hear the short man yell back at the other man. "And the police checked here before we did. That taxi driver was bloody lying."

Then we are gone.

WEDNESDAY
4.41 p.m.

My heart is racing. My hands are shaking too hard to unlock the front door. When Bunny swings it open, I practically fall inside.

"They're here!" I manage to gasp. "That was them."

"Who, Archie? Who were they?" Bunny urges. Little Tony is wrapped up in her arms and they both look frightened. Tony's lips are wobbling and his eyes are shining as he stares at me. Bunny's eyes fix on me too until she suddenly seems to snap into a decision, turning quickly to carry Little Tony through to the living room. I hear the burst of cartoons from the TV then she is back in the hall.

I am still leaning against the wall, my mind spinning, and she half carries me into the kitchen and drops me on to a chair.

"What's going on? Were they looking for you?"

I'm too shocked to reply. Despite the bright sunshine outside I feel icy cold.

Fear pours across Bunny's face. "Do you think they found this place?"

For a moment, a feeling of sheer terror floods through me before I calm slightly and slump back down in the seat.

"No." I shake my head. "When I left this morning I scattered some stones in front of the front door. They haven't been disturbed."

Bunny is pacing around the room, her eyes flicking between me and the door. Then she stops. "So who were those men and how do you know them?"

"I recognised them. They were with the person who shot my mother."

I say it calmly and bluntly but as I do, the memories flare in me again. The cracked face of the clock, the sound of the vase hitting the floor, the smell of gunpowder, the deafening shot and the look in her eyes. The pain and the surprise and then that horrible, practical understanding that has burned itself into my memory. And I am there again. Drowning in the feeling of helplessness.

"Archie!" Bunny is shaking me. "Archie," she shouts, and I slowly focus back on her. She looks scared and I wonder how long she has been saying my name.

She takes my hand. "Archie," she says. "This is getting out of control. You never said she was shot!"

I look at her. The room is still around us. I can hear birds singing outside and cars in the distance, on the road. The air is warm and heavy and dust particles glitter in the light that spills through the wide window.

"I don't talk about it," I say. "But they shot her, trying to steal that necklace. The Earl of Stafford is her cousin and the Madagascan diamonds are part of his collection. She borrowed the necklace to wear when my dad got his bravery award two years ago but then she was killed." I rub my face with my hands. "When Dad gave it back to the Earl he told him to get rid of it but he refused. Dad started saying it was cursed and it should be destroyed but everyone just laughed at him. That's the only reason why he might have gone and taken it..."

"What happened?" she asks.

"Three of them burst in just after Mum and Dad got back, although Dad thought no one knew she was going to wear the necklace. They forced their way in with masks on and tried to take it." I shrug. "There was a fight. A gun went off. She died."

"But you saw them?"

"I was sitting at the top of the stairs waiting for Mum and Dad to come home but I came down when it all happened and I saw it. The short one had a gun but Dad knocked it out of his hand. One of the others picked it up. The smallest one. It might have been a woman.

"Dad punched the tall one and his mask slipped for a moment. Before he hit Dad back, Dad crashed into the woman with the gun and it went off. Mum was standing in the wrong place."

I tell it like I told the police but the words don't seem real. In my mind, I can hear Dad phoning for an ambulance. Then Mum's voice as she reaches out to me. I feel the carpet under my knees as I kneel down to see her face. I watch her lips as she mouths my name, and look into her blue eyes, which are watery, glistening like they do sometimes when she's been laughing hard.

She smiles, then pulls me close to her. I can feel her warmth as she holds me for the last time.

"I love you, Archie," she whispers. "And I love your father. He's a good man. Look after him, won't you?"

And then she's gone.

Bunny listens to me tell it in silence.

"And they never caught them?" she says.

"I told them about the guy's scar but they didn't seem to take me seriously. And they never found any other evidence to identify them," I say. "Dad almost went crazy. Said there should have been some but he wasn't allowed to work on the case..."

I don't finish. Bunny crosses her arms hard across her body. "This is getting out of hand!" she hisses. "There are murderers after you. My brother is with us!" She waves her arms in the direction of the noise from the TV. "If you hadn't changed the way you looked, or if that man had been a bit more switched on, God knows what could have happened. This needs to stop now."

She is deadly serious, but she isn't right.

"Take Little Tony home," I say. "I'm sorry you were with me, but I need to carry on. When those men broke into our house we figured it was just ordinary thugs trying to steal the diamonds, but now we know there's something bigger happening. Carmichael and Radcliffe are involved and it's much more complicated. If Dad's in jail, I'm the only one who can work it out and stop them. If I don't, I'm going to lose him too."

And when I say it, I know that's what matters. I remember Dad screaming down the phone at the forensics team. I remember the tears. I remember my grandmother sitting so still and telling me I should go with them and her anger when I said no. I remember when Dad had to come and get me because I threw all the stuff off the supermarket shelves because I couldn't remember what we needed.

"I need to carry on," I say, and I feel more determined than ever. "His hearing's in less than two days. I need to get him out."

Bunny stares at me. I can't tell if the expression on her face is sad or angry or somewhere in between, but before she can say anything Little Tony sticks his head around the door.

"Can I have a drink, please?" he says quietly. Then he just stands there staring at us.

"OK, Treacle," Bunny says with a forced smile. "You go and sit back down, and I'll bring you one through."

He nods then trots off again.

"Dad would never have anything to do with killers," she says quietly. "Archie, this is scary."

"I know," I say. "I just need to understand how it's all linked."

She nods. "So what are you going to do?"

"I'm going to go to that party and have a good look around. If I can work it out and find some evidence, I can go to the police."

She grunts as if she's still not sure it's a good idea. Before she can say anything there is a beep of a horn from outside.

"That's my mum," she says. "I need to get going. Let me know if you need anything."

It feels wrong, leaving the conversation like this. "Bunny, wait," I say. "You've done enough. You can walk away. Just like your dad said you should."

But she just shakes her head. "No, Archie," she says. "I'm in this too now, aren't I?" She turns away and wipes her hand across her eyes. "I want you to help your dad. I wish someone had helped mine when he first needed it. I can't spend the rest of my life wishing I'd given him one last chance. If your dad's helping mine, maybe helping you is how I do that."

She sighs, then the determined look fixes itself back on her face. "You'd better get ready," she says. "That party isn't going to enjoy itself."

WEDNESDAY
6.54 p.m.

I end up rushing to get dressed. My clothes are filthy from where I slid down the conservatory roof earlier so I have to wait for the dry cleaners to shut to get more. Then I'm running late so I just grab the first suit that looks like it'll fit and the first dark tie I see. It's wrapped in a paper sleeve, and I don't look at it until I get back. And I don't expect it to be black.

I stand in front of the mirror, struggling to tie it, while the memories pulse in my mind. Needing help with the knot. Coming out on to the landing looking for someone and hearing the arguing. I remember the words feeling like weights on my shoulders, crushing me as I sat on my step, staring at the photograph and listening as my grandmother spilled out her anger.

"If you hadn't left the party so late... If you hadn't been drinking... You might have reacted quicker... You're supposed to be a policeman... My daughter would not be dead."

And then the hundred faces in the church, staring at me like they wanted to own my soul.

I loosen the tie then start again. Bunny's right that everyone will be smartly dressed and I wouldn't have thought of it myself, but as I struggle to tie it again, there's a knot of fear inside me that seems to spread out from my chest to my fingers, as if they are not under my control at all. I stare at myself in the mirror, trying to remind myself that I'm doing this for Dad and I need to keep going.

I'm the only chance he's got.

WEDNESDAY
8.19 p.m.

It takes me almost an hour to cycle the winding country lanes to Lakehurst Manor, but eventually I reach the two stone gateposts that guard a long gravelled drive to a large three-storey rectangular house. I keep going, pedalling hard around the wide perimeter until I reach the small wooded area to the side of the house that I saw on the satellite images online. I stop and check there is no one around before lifting the bike over the fence and scrambling after it, pushing through the thick undergrowth away from the road. Within seconds, I am hidden in the trees.

As I get closer to the house, the raucous sound of a party reaches me and I creep forward the last few metres, crouching low until I can peer out. In front of me I can see the back of the house behind a wide expanse of lawn. A bright-white marquee is pitched on the grass and there's a large gas-fired barbecue outside it. People are milling around, sitting at tables or standing in the sunshine clutching glasses and laughing loudly.

And then I see Carmichael in the middle of a group, waving his arms wildly as he tells a story before draining his glass and holding it out for a refill from a young waiter wearing black trousers, a white shirt and a smart black waistcoat. Keeping my eyes on him, I dump my bike and bag in some heavy undergrowth then dart around fifty metres northwards, until I am at the side of the house. For a moment, there is no one around. And I step out quickly into the sunshine.

Waiters and waitresses come and go down a pretty stone pathway that leads to a kitchen garden. They are busy and no one challenges me as I follow them to a wide gravelled area where two catering vans are parked. I stare around quickly, watching as the serving team unload prepared food from the vans then turn and take it back out to the marquee. To the side a girl with curly black hair is opening bottles of champagne and filling glasses on the table in front of her. I march up to her and smile awkwardly.

"I'm late," I say. "I need a waistcoat."

She looks up and I point to her waistcoat, which has an image of a top hat on the lapel and the words

Top Hat Catering underneath it.

"Where do you get it from?" I say again. "I got held up and I'll be in trouble if they find out."

She points at one of the vans. "There are some in the back." Then she smiles at me. "Don't worry," she says. "I won't tell if you don't," and she quickly takes a sip from one of the glasses before topping it up. "Then you can come back and take this tray out."

There are a bunch of waistcoats on a hook in the back of the van and I put one on then take the tray and march round to the garden again.

Just in time to see Carmichael talking to the taller one of my mum's killers.

Carmichael doesn't look happy. He is trying not to shout, but I can tell from his body language that he is furious. He clearly doesn't want to be having this conversation in public because he places his hand on the man's shoulder and leads him away from the group, then points back to the house.

They start walking towards me.

As they walk past, I keep my eyes down and hold out the tray I'm carrying. The tall man ignores me but Carmichael reaches out without looking at me and places his empty glass on it, then takes another one.

173

"At least she had the good sense not to come through," he snaps.

The other man's voice is deep and smooth like rich chocolate. "She said you could talk in the car," he says. "It's parked—"

"If you think I'm going to sit in the back of a car outside my own house while these important people come and go, you're mad," Carmichael interrupts. "We can meet in my study; we won't be disturbed."

The big man tenses, then seems to consider it. He shrugs and looks around for a minute while I turn and start to walk off, keeping my face away from him as I carry my tray towards the party, watching half over my shoulder as he follows the garden around the side of the house to the front drive.

A woman gestures with an empty glass then takes a step towards me to put it on the tray. She leans across to take a new one, then grabs the tray instinctively as I shove it towards her and force it into her hands. I ignore her startled expression. "There's a problem," I say, then I turn and run towards the house. "I'm very sorry."

I don't wait for a reply. I am running now, back towards the house, through the rear doors and into a huge kitchen. A few waiters and waitresses buzz around but I ignore them and go straight into a wide passageway that leads to the hall. The front door is half open but I don't have time to look out as I can hear steps on the gravel and Carmichael's voice coming towards me. To my left there are two doors and I open them quickly and stare through into huge empty living rooms. I turn back and dart past the wide staircase to a small corridor that leads to a heavy oak door. Just as the front door swings open.

I don't know if it's the study or not and I don't have time to check. The door is locked but my lock picks are already in my hands and I open it quickly, closing it behind me and locking it again just as Carmichael's voice booms out behind me.

"We can talk in here," he says. "And then you can go."

I look around frantically. I'm in a richly decorated room with expensive-looking paintings on the walls and shelves covered in smart leather-bound books. Two maroon leather sofas face each other on one side of the room while at the other side there is an enormous wooden desk, which is bare except for a closed laptop. Behind the desk is a smart leather chair.

I hear a key scratch clumsily against a lock and now I am trapped. The curtains are pulled back so the only place to hide is under the desk. For a moment I feel like my body is frozen. If I'm caught there will be no way to escape, but I don't seem to have a choice. I duck down and cram myself into the small, dark space between the edge of the desk and an old metal safe, just in time to hear the key turn in the lock and the door swing open.

I hear a woman's voice, harsh and full of contempt. I can't see but I can hear as she practically pushes Carmichael into the room then slams the door behind her. Carmichael is trying to be strong, but this woman is clearly the boss. Carmichael doesn't seem to like it.

"And now you dare threaten me in my own house!" he says, his voice slurred with drink. "You come down here, interrupt my party, just to tell me what I already know?" Carmichael pauses and I figure they're standing close together. "It wasn't so long ago you were the junior constable making me cups of tea when I was robbed," he snarls.

Her reply is icy. "I might have been the junior

constable, but it was me who worked out that the robbery was faked," she says. "If I'd opened my mouth you would have got two years in prison for insurance fraud."

She's not going to back down and Carmichael seems to realise it. There is the sound of a bottle being opened and the splash of liquid in a glass before I hear the creak of the sofas as they both sit down.

"Look, Carmichael," she says harshly. "I rely on you to control things down here. If I can't..." She lets the words hang in the air.

Carmichael seems to know what they mean and he answers sharply. "You can rely on me." Then he gulps at his drink, which steadies him. "Of course you can rely on me."

"Good. Because I want you to take the stones back for a day or two."

Carmichael seems to splutter. "Haven't you found that damn kid yet? You said you had it under control."

"It is under control," the woman says firmly. Then she hesitates. "We'll find him soon, I'm sure."

I know she's talking about me and for a moment I feel a strange thrill that I have managed to beat them for this long. Except they are just a few paces away and if they find me there's no way I can escape.

"So why don't *you* keep them?" Carmichael says

"I'm a serving police officer, for God's sake. I can't just wander around with them."

My breath catches in my throat. No wonder Dad said we couldn't trust the police. I wonder how complicated their scheme is and how many robberies they are responsible for. I bet she wouldn't think twice about getting rid of me if I get in her way. Suddenly I feel sick just thinking about it.

There is a creak of the sofa as they stand. The room darkens slightly and I figure they are standing in front of the window but I don't know why. Carmichael whistles slightly and now I have a desperate urge to know what they're doing. With my heart in my mouth, I stretch out on the floor behind the desk until I can almost see into the room. Then I stretch out a little further.

And my blood runs cold.

They are standing with their backs to me in front of the window, each of them holding a large square Madagascan diamond up to the light. I recognise the stones, even though they must have been removed from the necklace, but I don't understand how they could have got them. The necklace is hidden back at the house, isn't it? Half of me wants to burst out from where I am hiding to go and check, but I can't. I force myself to be calm for just a few more minutes.

I can't see the woman and I wonder if I edge out from the desk, whether I'll be able to see her face, but before I can move they have gone back to the sofas and there's no way I can see without revealing myself. The woman starts speaking again.

"Keep them safe for a few days and I'll tell you when I need them, OK?" she says. Her tone turns harder again. "And listen, Carmichael," she adds. "This is the last one so don't screw it up. Blake is in court in two days and after he gets sent down the file will be shut and we'll be in the clear. We'll sell the diamonds and that will be it."

"Why does it have to be the last one?" Carmichael asks, but this seems to be the wrong thing to say.

There is the sound of a glass being slammed on a table. "Do you realise how close Blake got?" she hisses. "He was investigating Radcliffe's, for God's sake. He put in an application for a search warrant! Fortunately, I managed to ensure the paperwork went missing before it reached the judge. Do you think Radcliffe would hold up to an interrogation?"

There's a pause while she seems to calm herself. "Look," she says. "Even with Blake out of the way this scheme has run its course. Get Radcliffe to go through everything he's got and destroy anything that might be incriminating. With no evidence we're in the clear. I want to talk to the others and lay out a few ground rules about how this ends first thing in the morning, so find somewhere neutral for us to meet."

"And what about Blake?"

"I've wrapped so much evidence around him he'll have to be remanded at the hearing. Prison isn't a safe place. Especially as I've arranged for him to have an ... accident."

Her words stab through me like a knife. This woman has got the diamonds and now she's talking about killing my dad. I want to charge out and attack them but they are two adults and those thugs are probably right outside the door. The only chance my dad's got is if I can get enough evidence against them so people have to believe me. Which means I can't afford to get caught. I squeeze my eyes shut and sit as still as I can.

There is another creak of leather as they both get up. I sense their footsteps on the thick carpet as they walk towards the door until they stop. The woman seems to be waiting for something.

"Aren't you going to put them in the safe?" she asks eventually.

"What?"

"The safe," she repeats. "Don't you have a safe in here?"

Panic grips me. Because I am leaning on the safe. And there's nowhere else I can go. All I can do is get ready to run.

Carmichael seems to hesitate. "I, um…" he starts. "The combination's written down upstairs," he murmurs. "I'll have to go and get it."

There's a pause and when the woman speaks again her voice is full of menace. "Do it!" she orders. "No more mistakes! I've risked everything to get here, Carmichael," she spits. "So don't screw up and don't cross me."

Her voice is like ice as it drips through my ears and makes its way down my spine. Carmichael comes over to the desk and for a terrible moment I think he's remembered the combination, but he hasn't. He just puts down his glass and moves away again.

Then, finally, they leave the room.

WEDNESDAY
9.04 p.m.

When the door closes, I feel my body buckle and my shoulders start to shake. I drag myself out from under the desk and lean back against it, breathing heavily with my elbows resting on my knees and my head lowered. That woman was talking about murder like it was nothing and I don't know how, but somehow they've got the diamonds. I feel like there are too many thoughts swimming around in my head to concentrate, and Carmichael will be back any minute. I need to get out of here and talk to Bunny.

I can't hear anything at the door so I silently open it and stride out. Keeping my head down, I march through the hall, into the kitchen then out into the garden. Carmichael is coming back around the house from the front but I turn my face and ignore him, walking quickly across the stone path towards the trees at the side of the house, unbuttoning my waistcoat as I walk, taking my phone out of my pocket and calling

Bunny's number. As I get into the trees, she answers.

"Bunny, they've got the diamonds," I say quickly. "They must have found the necklace in the house and taken it."

"They can't have."

"They have. And they're going to kill my dad. And the woman in charge of everything's a police officer. She ruined my dad's investigation and framed him."

"Archie, slow down," Bunny urges. "Start at the beginning. What makes you think they've got the diamonds?"

I move further into the trees then drop down into the undergrowth and stare back at the house, trying to organise my thoughts. "I saw them, Bunny. They had two of the diamonds from the necklace. I'd know them anywhere. I know I said I didn't have them but—"

She interrupts. "Just hold on a second, will you? I'm at Dad's house. I'll go next door and check."

From outside the marquee, a roar of laughter rises up into the air and it seems so out of place it shocks me. Then after a few seconds Bunny comes back on to the line.

"Archie, you're wrong," she says. "They're still here. You must have seen something else."

"But I didn't —" I start, then I catch myself. "You didn't even know I had them. How do you know they're still there?"

Something flashes in my mind and maybe Bunny can hear it in my tone because when she speaks again her voice is cold.

"Don't you dare think about suspecting me of something," she starts. "Everyone knows you had that necklace," she says. "And hiding the *ice* in the ice box is so unoriginal even my little brother wouldn't do it. I found them within seconds of you first going into the roof. And I could have taken them, but I didn't. I just moved them somewhere safer."

"Where did you put them?"

"Dad's got a few little hiding places that no one would find. Don't worry. They're safe."

Guilt rushes through me and I wonder how I could have doubted her. "I'm sorry," I say. "I should have told you."

"Yes, you should." Then her tone eases. "But the necklace is still here and nobody's touched it. So you must have seen something else."

"Fakes?"

"I doubt it," she says. "You might be fooled by a

fake but anyone who knows anything can spot them pretty easily. Especially with stones that size."

I stare out at the house while I think. Out in front of me, Carmichael has another drink in his hand and I wonder how long the party will go on for. "If they're not fakes," I say, "they must be real. And if they're real there's only one explanation that makes any sense. But we need to get hold of them to check."

"What are you going to do?" Bunny asks.

I check the time, then think about the kit I brought from the house. "I'm going to steal them," I say. "Then we'll finally know. I'll meet you at your dad's house when it's done."

Bunny hesitates. "OK," she says eventually. "But be careful. You've been lucky so far. You can't afford to get caught."

I take a deep breath. "We don't have time to be careful. I have to get those stones."

I cut the call and try to crush the rising sense of fear that's spreading throughout my body. At least I'm out here, I think to myself, and not in a prison cell. I urge my dad to hold on a little bit longer.

And pray that I can do the same.

THURSDAY
2.17 a.m.

The house looks different at night, especially through binoculars.

I've been waiting hours for the party to finish, hiding in the trees wearing my black clothes and a black ski mask, watching Carmichael as he enjoyed himself among the guests until eventually everyone left. I'm tired, but I force myself to focus on the second floor where a bathroom window has been left open. It's up high and Carmichael probably figures no one can get through it, but I reckon I can. I am tall but I am skinny, and more agile than most adults. And there've been no lights on that floor all night. So I figure it's the safest place to get inside.

I sprint across the ground, feeling the burning in my muscles after staying still for so long. Then I grip the old-fashioned metal drainpipe and start hauling myself up, hand over hand, using window ledges where I can, until finally I get to the window. I hold the frame and crouch on the ledge, enjoying the cool breeze as I rest for a moment to slow my heart rate before stretching up and sliding myself through. I twist my hips and roll forward, then listen for any sign of stirring in the house. But the night is silent apart from my slight panting.

I am in.

The tick of an old grandfather clock in the hall echoes through the night as I creep quickly down two sets of stairs to the study then open the locked door silently and duck inside. The room doesn't seem to have been touched since earlier so I push the heavy leather chair aside and crawl back under the desk, sitting cross-legged in front of the sixty-centimetre-square Chatswood Milner safe. The safe opens by turning a numbered wheel four times alternately left and right to a set combination, but with the kit I've got I reckon I can open it. Holding my torch in my teeth, I open a sleek grey box and take out a wire around a metre long with a tiny microphone on one end and a set of headphones on the other. Then I measure the distance between the wheel and the edge of the safe's door with a tape measure and carefully stick the microphone to a point exactly one third of the way across with a piece of black tape. Finally I put on the headphones and turn them on.

With the silence in the house, it's easy to hear the safe's internal noises as I turn the dial. The *click, click, click* seems as loud as a drum and soon I hear the solid *thunk* as the tumbler falls and I get the first number. And within a minute I have found them all.

Inside the safe there are two levels. The bottom is piled with papers, cheque books, old-looking documents and other stuff, but I am not interested in any of that. On the shelf above is a single black leather box. As I grab it, a sudden sense of urgency floods through me and I can feel my fingers trembling. I pause and shake my head to clear it, then take a deep breath. I twist the catch and the box springs open.

Gold necklaces, rings and coins glow warmly in the weak light of the torch, but I just want the diamonds so I dump them on the floor and check the box again. In the middle there is a tassel so I tug at it and a false bottom lifts to reveal an empty velvet-lined cavity below. I stare at it, then tip the box over in my hands and frantically spread everything I have taken out of the safe on the floor in front of me. But it is no use.

The diamonds aren't there.

I don't understand. That woman ordered Carmichael to lock them in the safe, so they should be here – unless Carmichael really couldn't remember the combination. Maybe he didn't have it written down somewhere, or maybe he forgot or just couldn't be bothered to go back and lock them up. In which case...

I rock back on my heels, feeling like the room is spinning around me, trying to think back through the evening. When I came out of the house earlier, I saw Carmichael go straight into the garden. So even though he promised to put them in the safe, he must have still had the diamonds in his pocket. And I've been watching him all night. He hasn't been back inside since.

I close my eyes and go through it again but now I think about it, I'm sure. After the last guests left, I watched the lights in the house flick on and off as he went to bed: garden lights, kitchen lights, hall and then the bedroom on the far right at the rear of the house. But none of the other rooms and definitely not the study. So the only place the diamonds could be is in his bedroom.

I take a deep breath. And wish things could be simple.

I creep to the first floor, glad of the thick carpet that keeps me quiet, then kneel outside the last door on the rear side of the landing and take a wire-thin endoscopic camera out of another grey case. I poke the thin black camera wire through the keyhole and plug the other end into a hand-held screen, staring at it for a moment as I get the hang of the weird images through the tiny lens. Now I can see around the room.

He didn't care about the mess when he went to bed. Carmichael's jacket and trousers are on the floor in the corner of the room and now he is asleep, breathing heavily.

I twist the wire to see around, trying to work out where the diamonds might be, but there is nowhere obvious and the only option I've got is to go in and search for them. I can feel the pressure building inside me again but I crush it down, then pull the wire back through the keyhole and grip the handle of the heavy oak door. I open it silently, then crouch on my hands and knees to crawl through the doorway, around to the bedside table, but there is nothing. With my heart in my mouth, I slide open the drawer, but again there is nothing and now I'm running out of ideas. There is a dressing table but it's clear and doesn't have any drawers. The only other places to look are a large walk-in wardrobe, which could take hours to search properly, and the en suite bathroom. I am just summoning up the courage to crawl into the wardrobe when I look again at Carmichael's suit jacket, which has been dropped on the floor. Maybe if he couldn't be bothered to put the diamonds in the safe, he couldn't be bothered to take them out of his pocket. Pulling the jacket towards me, I search through it quickly, then almost cheer as my fingers close around the two hard diamonds that have been left loose with a packet of mints and a wad of tissues. As I take them out, I pause, watching as even in this darkness, the diamonds seem to send sparkles of light around the room. As I drop them into a cloth bag, Carmichael sleeps on and I turn to leave.

Except before I reach the door, there is a groan from the bed and a snort as Carmichael seems to choke himself awake. I freeze, and flatten myself against the floor, urging him in my mind to go back to sleep, but he doesn't. It gets worse. Carmichael swings himself to the side of the bed and starts to get up.

I push myself as far down as I can, forcing

myself flat on to the carpet, hiding in the shadow, concentrating on trying to keep my breathing quiet as my heart races. Carmichael stands up groggily. His feet hit the carpet hard next to the bed then move along the floor, no more than centimetres from my head. He opens the door to the bathroom and I hear the bump of the toilet seat being lifted before he answers the call of nature. As the splashing continues, I take my chance. I crawl quickly back to the door and through it. When the toilet flushes I pull the door shut and creep away from the room.

Within minutes I am out in the garden and back at the spot where I left my bike. I pull out my phone and text Bunny.

Wake up. I've got them. Meet me back at number 17

Then I ride as fast as I can to the house.

When I get back, the sun is rising and Bunny is waiting in the grey light. I don't say anything but pass her the stones then lead the way up to the attic. Bunny sits and drops them on the desk, turning on an extra lamp and grabbing a magnifying glass before staring at them carefully for a long time. Then she leans back and looks at me over her shoulder.

"You were right," she says. "Now what are we going to do?"

THURSDAY
6.04 a.m.

"So they are real?"

Bunny nods. "Yeah," she says. "But low quality."

I take the Madagascan necklace out of its box and pass it to her. "And these are much better?"

Bunny takes it and examines the stones. "Two of them," she says. "The others aren't great."

"Show me."

Bunny holds them up and for a moment we just stare as the early morning light dances off the diamonds. She turns them over in her hand and sparkles of light spin around the room as if she is holding a glitter ball. I am enchanted, until Bunny's voice breaks the moment.

"First," she says, "look at the colour. These two stones in the necklace have no colour at all. They are bright white." She takes one of the loose diamonds and places it next to one of the stones from the necklace. They are both the same size and shape and

I can't see any difference.

"So are these, aren't they?"

Bunny shakes her head. "Close, but not quite. The diamonds Carmichael had are a couple of shades off. A little closer to grey."

She picks up a pencil and points at parts of the loose diamonds. "Most diamonds have flaws," she goes on, "but the best quality have the fewest and smallest flaws so that they can hardly be seen. If you use the magnifying glass on these, you can clearly see blemishes."

I look through the magnifying glass and I can see she is right. In the loose stones there are a number of tiny smudges. When I look at the stones in the necklace there are less and in one stone there are none.

"Last," she says, "the quality of the stone is affected by the cut, or the way the cutter has turned the diamond from a rough lump that came out of the ground into this shape."

I lean closer but I can't see a difference. "They look the same to me," I say.

Bunny nods thoughtfully. "Yeah. Not bad, are they? They've done a good job in cutting these."

I hesitate before asking what I really want to know. "So what's the difference in value?"

Bunny picks up one of the loose diamonds. "This stone weighs just over nine carats. It's worth over two hundred grand."

"Wow," I say. It's just a small bit of clear rock. And it's worth as much as a house. It doesn't seem right.

Bunny just smiles. "What do you think this one is worth?" she asks, pointing at the best of the necklace stones.

I don't know so I shrug. "More, I guess."

"About a million."

And suddenly I feel afraid to touch it. I drop it on the table and step back. "So how much is the whole necklace worth?" I ask.

"Well over four million quid."

I sit on the floor with my back against the wall and there is silence for a minute as I try to reason things through in my mind. Eventually I turn to Bunny. "Everyone on the list of names my dad had was burgled," I say, "but for some reason the thieves never got away with the jewels, right?"

"Right," Bunny says. "Or that's what people thought."

"But they were wrong, weren't they?" I say. "The burglars never meant to take the jewels. They just removed the best stones and replaced them with low-quality ones bought from Israel and cut to the same size and shape by Radcliffe."

"Exactly," says Bunny. "They're still genuine diamonds so no one suspects they've been switched. People would spot a fake, but these are real. And because they're all historical pieces, the real value of the necklace or the earrings or whatever is in the history and the story, not the stones it's made with. It doesn't matter what quality the stones are so no one really checks. It's more important that they came from the court of Henry the Seventh or the neck of Joséphine Bonaparte."

I think back to the silver cufflinks that were so much more valuable than the gold ones at the auction and I know she's right. Then I stare at the ceiling of the little room, trying to imagine how they did it. Carmichael would find historical pieces with high-value stones in them. Radcliffe would buy cheaper stones from Israel and cut them in the same shape. Then the thugs would break into a country house and switch the stones without anybody realising.

"It's brilliant," I say. "Nothing valuable seems to go missing. No one is looking for the original stones. They must have made a fortune."

Bunny nods. "Dad always says historical pieces are way overpriced. You can't flog stories on the black market."

She is buzzing and I realise I am too, until I think about Dad and my thoughts crash back to reality. "They must have been targeting the Madagascan necklace after they failed the time before. My dad got hold of it before they could do the switch," I say. "But they knew he was on to them and they framed him. The person in charge is a police officer so she figured she could switch the stones when they arrested him."

"But he didn't have them; you did!" Bunny says. Then she seems to hesitate. "I wonder how my dad was helping your dad?"

I try to smile. "If he knew half of what you know he'd have been pretty useful."

She beams at me for a moment, then we sit in silence.

Bunny looks up. "Why don't we go to the police now?" she says, but I shake my head.

"We still don't have any evidence. We can't prove

they've robbed anyone. We can't prove anything. Who's going to believe us?"

"What about the diamonds? Isn't four million quid's worth of evidence enough?"

"All they've done is buy new diamonds and cut them. They haven't switched them yet. The only thing illegal is me stealing them." I run my hands over my face. "And the only way to get evidence is to find out where they're meeting today and go and take it."

"How do we do that?"

I shrug. "I don't know," I say, and suddenly I feel so tired I can't think straight. I've been up all night and cycled about forty miles. I am dirty from lying on the ground and somehow I've managed to tear my shirt and cut my wrist. Dad's in court tomorrow and I know I need to do something, but all I want to do is sleep.

Bunny suddenly straightens. "I've got it!" she says, leaning down and slapping my cheeks with both her hands.

I groan. "Go on."

"We don't know where they're meeting, but we know *who's* going to the meeting. Why don't we wait outside one of their houses until we see them leave, then follow them? They said they would meet first thing, but it's still early. We might not have missed them."

It's a brilliant idea and I feel the energy pour back into me. "Let's get to Radcliffe's now," I say. "There's a café we can watch from. We need to get you a bike."

Bunny shakes her head. "Cycling might take too long. What if we miss them? Let's take a taxi."

"We haven't got enough money."

A smile creeps over the corners of Bunny's mouth and turns slowly into a grin as she reaches into her pocket and pulls out a big wad of fifty-pound notes. "I found them in Dad's hiding place when I was moving your necklace. I reckon he must have forgotten about them."

I stare at her. "Is there anything else I should know about?" I say, before quickly holding up my hands and shaking my head. "Don't tell me," I add. "Let's just get going."

Bunny grins. "We do need to hurry," she says, "but you can't go out looking like some sort of junior assassin. Have a shower and get changed while I ring for a cab."

I have just got out of the shower when she shouts up to tell me the taxi's here. I get dressed and grab my phone then race downstairs. Bunny is outside, holding the car door open for me, so I get in and slide across. She slides in next to me and the driver turns to check we are both in.

I recognise him immediately. Because he is the man who picked me up from Brighton station.

THURSDAY
7.38 a.m.

I stare at the back of the taxi driver's head and don't say anything. We don't have time to call for another cab and, anyway, I look pretty different. I got in quickly and am right behind him so maybe he won't recognise me, but I feel the unease creep through my guts as I let Bunny give instructions to go to Radcliffe's jewellery shop. Criminals make mistakes, Dad says, and I've done it. I wonder how I could be so stupid.

The streets are clear, and we arrive in a few minutes. I get out and walk down the lane to the back of the shop. When Bunny catches up with me I ask her how she found the driver.

"I used the card by the front door," she says. "Why? Is it a problem?"

I should have thrown it away but I didn't and now Bunny's looking at me like she's done something wrong, but it's not her fault. "Probably not," I say. "I was surprised, that's all."

The café is just opening and we are about to sit down when Radcliffe appears, striding purposefully through his back door down the steps and towards the alley. We watch as he climbs into a small red VW Golf and I know we have moments before he has gone. The only way to follow him now is to use the taxi we came in and Bunny waves it down just before it leaves. She scrambles inside and holds the door for me, and again I feel like I've got no choice but to get in.

Bunny leans forward. "Follow that car," she says to the driver.

The driver turns in his seat. "Are you serious?"

"Yes," Bunny replies.

"But don't get too close," I add, and immediately wish I hadn't.

The driver twists round to look at me. "What's going on, lad?" he asks.

"It's a game," I say. "Like a treasure hunt." Though it sounds lame and I look away.

I can feel his eyes on me for a few more moments and he seems about to say something, then changes his mind and starts the engine.

"Whatever you say, son," he says. "You're paying."

Two minutes later Radcliffe pulls into the car park of an empty sports ground. The taxi drops us a little further on and drives off while we go back, arriving in time to see Radcliffe park near Carmichael's Aston Martin, then walk towards an old wooden changing room on the side of the pitch. The path he is going down is in the open so we can't follow, but there is a hedge all the way around the pitch and if we circle round we can get much closer from the other side. I whisper to Bunny to follow then race round to see him through a gap in the hedge as he reaches the door and goes in. Before the door shuts, I can see there are already several other figures inside.

I turn to Bunny. "I've got to go and find out what they're saying."

She stares through the gap. "There's nowhere to hide down there. Wait till they come out."

I shake my head. "We'll miss it. I need to find out what they're talking about. You stay here and keep your eyes open. I'll put my phone on vibrate. If there's any trouble, get out of here and I'll see you back at the house."

She doesn't look happy, but she nods and squeezes herself into the hedge so she can't be seen from either the path or the pitch. Then I run as fast as I can over the grass, sliding to a stop at the back of the old wooden changing rooms and holding my breath for several seconds. But there is no movement and the door stays closed. They haven't noticed.

The windows at the back of the building are too high to see through but in the stillness of the field I can hear people arguing inside. The short man we almost bumped into yesterday is speaking.

"I don't see why we should stop now," he says. "These are easy jobs. We should carry on."

But the next voice is the woman and she isn't interested. "It's over, and that's final. We all need to be back doing our day jobs by tomorrow. My lot will turn up the necklace eventually, then I'll find a way to switch the diamonds. We'll sell them and you'll get your share. I've got other plans I want to move on to."

"Things that don't include us, I suppose?" Carmichael grunts.

"Things that don't include anyone." She hesitates as if waiting for someone to speak, but no one does. "And if you're too greedy to accept it; if you gamble away your money too quickly and think about looking up your old pals for a loan..." She pauses. "Or if I ever even hear your names again, you will end up in jail or you'll end up dead."

The threat is stark and has an immediate effect on the room. There is a pause before Radcliffe speaks.

"I'll be glad it's over. I never wanted much to do with it in the first place."

"Pleased enough with the money though, weren't you?" Carmichael's smug voice rings out. "Pleased enough to bail out that failing business of yours. How many years did your shop lose money for before we came along?"

"We should have stopped after that woman got killed."

"Once she was dead it was too late," says Carmichael.

The woman's voice cuts in again. "But we're stopping now and that's the end of it. Once you get your money there'll be nothing to tie us together."

She is interrupted by the sound of a phone ringing, and the room stops. Then I hear the smooth voice of the tall thug, like honey being poured over chocolate.

"Yes."

There's a pause and the room waits before the voice speaks again. "Thank you very much for calling.

Yes, we are still looking for him."

Pause.

"Really? You picked him up where? And where did you take him? That's really helpful. My sister will be so relieved to hear that. At least we know he's safe. And please do call if you see him again. I'll make it worth your while."

I close my eyes for a moment as a wave of fear washes over me. I know that was the taxi driver on the end of the phone and the call was about me. I stand up, aware that the room has gone silent. My phone buzzes in my pocket and I whip it out. It's Bunny but I only have time to hear her scream, "They're coming," when the two thugs burst out around the side of the changing rooms and trap me between them.

I try to run but they rugby-tackle me and force me hard against the wooden wall of the building, smashing my shoulder into the panelling and forcing the breath from my lungs. My phone tumbles out of my hand into a gap between the floor of the building and the ground, but before I can grab it they have twisted my arm behind my back, forcing me to cry out in pain.

"Well, well, well," the smaller man says. "We've been

looking for you."

He is pulling hard on my arm like he's going to rip it out of its socket, but the other man stops him. "Don't break his arm yet, Conran," he says. "Let's see what she wants to do with him first."

Conran grunts and relaxes his grip a little as he forces me through the wooden door and into the away team's dressing room.

Where the others are waiting.

Carmichael is standing in the far corner next to Radcliffe, who is sitting on the hard wooden bench with his head in his hands. And at the back of the room, sitting on the bench beneath the captain's peg, is the woman who is running the show.

The woman who killed my mother.

She has medium-length brown hair and a rather plain face with no jewellery or make-up. She looks about average height, dressed in jeans and a simple white T-shirt, and she could be aged anywhere between thirty and fifty. She sits completely still, looking like any other woman you might pass in the street and not think twice about, except when you see her eyes, which are cold and dark and sad.

This is the woman who has destroyed my family.

She stares at me, then smiles, a strange, scared tightening of her lips that sends a chill down my spine. "Hello, Archie," she says. "You look just like your mother."

Carmichael spins around. "How do you know his mother?" he says. Then his eyes fix on me. "He was at my auction. Who is this boy?"

"You idiot, Carmichael. It's Blake's son. Look at the photo."

She throws him a photograph and I can see it is the same one the police were using. Carmichael takes it and his eyes widen. Radcliffe looks at it and then at me.

"Someone broke into the shop but didn't take anything," he says. "Was it you?"

I don't answer.

Radcliffe continues nervously. "What are we going to do with him?"

"Harris," she barks at the taller of the two thugs. "Was he alone?"

Harris nods, and suddenly I feel more afraid than I thought was possible.

"I don't know anything about anything," I blurt out desperately.

But she knows better. "It doesn't matter what you know," she says. "It's too late. First of all, you know something. Secondly, you have seen us all together. Thirdly, if you ever have a chance to speak to your dad, I'm sure he would put it together." She shrugs. "So it's too late for you. Just like it's too late for your dad."

"What do you mean, it's too late for my dad?"

"Sit him down." She barks the order and I fight hard but Conran forces me on to the bench, leaning his weight on my shoulder so I can't move.

"You're going to kill Blake, aren't you?" Radcliffe says. "Or have him killed, I suppose."

She doesn't answer. Radcliffe reaches into a pocket and takes out a packet of cigarettes and some matches. He lights one and smokes nervously.

No one seems to have anything more to say and I don't know what to say either. I want to fight but Conran's leaning on my shoulder like he's going to crush me. She just pushes her hair back behind her ears and looks around.

"I think we all know where we stand. This is the end of it." She turns to Carmichael. "You may be needed to verify the piece when we have it back. Then wait the normal period, sell the diamonds and split the profit." She jabs a finger accusingly. "Don't spend it too quickly or it might get noticed. Don't become a nuisance and don't ever let me hear from you again." She walks over to the door and holds it open. "Now, get out."

I watch as Carmichael and Radcliffe troop to the door silently. As he leaves, Radcliffe turns towards her. "What's going to happen to the boy?"

She thinks for a moment before taking the matches from his hand and tossing them to Conran. Then she holds the door open for the jeweller to leave without answering his question.

And I am alone with the killers.

The two hard men are standing either side of me facing their boss as she comes forward.

"What do you know?" she asks, but I don't answer.

Suddenly her hand lashes out, slapping my face hard. "What do you know?" she hisses.

I stare at her and I feel my fear turn to anger. "I know you're a police officer," I say. "I know you set up my dad. And I know you're replacing valuable jewels with cheap ones for massive profits."

"How did you find us?"

211

"Carmichael made a payment to Radcliffe through his Israeli bank account. It wasn't hard."

"But how did you find Radcliffe?"

I don't answer. She raises his hand to strike me again but maybe she can tell it won't work as I just glare at her. Her expression doesn't change. She nods briefly and looks at Harris. "How do you think he found Radcliffe?"

Harris shrugs. "What about the middleman? Taylor? He knows everything that goes on in precious stones. Rumour is he wants to get out of the business."

She seems surprised by that. "You think that could be true?"

Harris nods. "Could be," he says.

She puffs out her cheeks and breathes out hard. "Blake was the arresting officer when he was last picked up."

Harris scratches his scar. "Maybe they did a deal," he says.

"Maybe," she agrees.

She turns her dark eyes back on to me. "OK, time's up," she says. "Where are the diamonds?"

I feel my jaw clench. "What diamonds?" I say.

And she almost laughs. "The diamonds your father

stole from Stafford House," she says. "The ones I told him were being targeted by your mum's killers. The ones he couldn't resist taking so he could set up a meeting and bring them to justice after all these years."

She says it in a mocking tone, like she's been one step ahead of everyone else for all this time, and maybe she has, but all she's doing is making me more determined.

She leans in close. "There's only one set of diamonds that's missing in all this, Archie. Now, where are they?"

She practically spits the last sentence at me, but I don't move and we stare at each other in silence until Conran raises his fist and smiles. "Want me to find out?" he asks.

She looks at the short man and seems to hesitate. "No," she says eventually. "We haven't got time. We need to silence him permanently and it needs to look like an accident. If they find any injuries on his body there'll be more questions." She pulls her phone out of her pocket. "The diamonds will turn up," she says. "When the police find them, we'll follow the original plan."

Silence me permanently.

I feel a stab of fear like ice down my back. "You're going to kill me, aren't you?" I gasp. "Just like you killed my mother."

She sighs and I flinch as she pats my cheek. "Poor Archie," she says. "I killed your mother, I framed your father and now I'm going to kill you. What is the world coming to?"

I lunge at her but Conran grabs my collar and shoves me hard into the wall so my shoulder explodes in pain. I kick at him, but he holds me at arm's length before throwing me into the wall again. Light flashes in my eyes, and when I open them again Conran has pulled back his fist to really hurt me, but she steps in.

"Conran!" she barks. "I told you. Not too much damage."

"Why are you doing this?" I say. "You're twisted!"

She looks stunned at the accusation, then she seems to sigh. "Life gets twisted, Archie," she says in a matter-of-fact way. "You think things will be straightforward then you make a mistake and all of a sudden, you're in trouble. Maybe it's gambling debts like Carmichael, or your business failing like Radcliffe's. Maybe you fall in love and you do a favour for someone you shouldn't..."

She shakes her head. "Whatever it might be," she continues, "sometimes you get into a position where you feel like you've got no choice but to do something terrible. So you do it and then maybe it didn't feel so terrible, so you do it some more. And before you know it, you're trapped and your career's ruined and the only thing to do is throw yourself into it as deep as you can because there's no way out.

"And if you don't believe it's that easy, just ask your dad," she says. "Or maybe you've worked it out for yourself over the last few days. You're on your own in this life," she adds. "The only way to survive is to look after yourself and let the world go to hell."

She turns away as she checks the screen on her phone and for a moment I wonder if she is right. I wonder how far my dad was prepared to go and how far I am. How far the desperation and fear will push me before there's no way back. I wonder if she was tricked or if she just made the wrong choices, and Taylor's words about spreading the sickness spring back to my mind. Then I shake my head. She is wrong about being on my own. There are people on my side and I'm on theirs. I'm going to get through this and put things right.

As long as she doesn't kill me first.

She puts the phone back in her pocket. "Make sure this place is secure," she says. "Check the locks on the windows. There was a padlock on the front door. Make sure it works. Conran, hold him still while Harris checks."

I wrestle against Conran's grip, but it's like a vice clamped on my shoulder.

"What are you going to do to me?" I scream.

"Shut you up. It will be a tragedy. A runaway boy killed in a fire while dossing down in a sports pavilion. This place is so dry it'll burn to the ground before anyone gets near; a tragic accident blamed on vandals. I'd keep the windows shut if I were you."

So I die of the smoke, not the flames, I think, and the full horror of what is going to happen hits me.

Harris comes back into the room. "Everything's secure, boss. He can't get out. There's padlocks on the doors and windows."

She nods. "Good. We need to get back. Conran, you know what to do."

She leaves the room and Harris follows, leaving me with Conran. The short man just laughs then shoves me hard so I stumble backwards, crashing forcefully on to the floor. Before I can recover, he leaves, slamming the door behind him. I run to the door, pounding on it with my fists, screaming at Conran to let me out, but it's useless.

I stop hammering and listen. For a minute I can hear crashing and splintering, followed by the rustle of paper and then the strike of a match. Then there is silence before the outer door opens and slams shut again. Conran has gone and I am trapped inside a tinder-dry wooden building.

Which he has set on fire.

Crackling sounds from outside the door are broken by irregular spitting as the wood burns. I spin round and stare at the room, which is rectangular with wooden floors and walls and an opening at the side that leads to the showers. At the back of the changing room there is a window and another at the back of the shower area, but they only open a few centimetres until they hit a wire mesh grille designed to stop the windows getting smashed by balls. The outer mesh frame is secured by a padlock on the outside. There's no way I can reach it from inside.

I race to the door and push against it as hard as I can but it is stuck fast, and now it's getting hot.

Smoke is rising through the gap under it so I run into the shower room and turn on all the showers before sprinting to the window to shout out as loudly as I can. I scream that I'm trapped. I yell until my breath has gone and my throat aches. But no one comes.

The door is now too hot to touch and smoke pours into the room. My lungs are burning, I am coughing continually and I don't know what else I can do. I am going to lose. There is no way to escape. I just run back to the showers and sit under the water.

Watching as the room fills up with smoke.

THURSDAY
8.19 a.m.

"Archie, wake up." The voice is screaming. Is it Dad? Or Mum? I want to sleep but the voice won't give up. "Archie," it screams. "Archie, you need to wake up."

I try to move but I have no strength. I lean on my hand, which slips on the tiles, and my face falls into the cold water. The shock wakes me and I take a breath. The air is cleaner down near the floor.

"Archie! Wake up!"

The voice is screaming – refusing to go away. I open my eyes and look to the window. The room is filled with thick smoke but I can see movement behind the glass. "Archie, get up," the voice orders. "Get up now!"

And something stirs in me. Help is here. If I can get up I might be able to get out. My lungs ache but I manage to drag myself to the window. It is still open as far as it will go, and the smoke is less thick.

"Come on, Archie, get up," the voice yells again.

It's Bunny.

I pull myself up and squeeze my face into fresh air, sucking in the clear emptiness. I can see her face, screaming at me. "I can't open the window; it's locked. I can't get the padlock off. Archie, you've got to help me get you out."

Behind me there is a roar, and the door and part of the wall burst into flames. The heat explodes on to my back, despite my soaked clothes, but I try to focus on Bunny. She is screaming something about a padlock. Padlocks are easy to open, aren't they?

"You need to pick the lock," I gasp, trying to wipe the smoke from my eyes.

But she just screams at me again, her voice furious. "I've never picked a lock in my life. You need to tell me how to do it."

I don't know if it's the fear in her voice or the few breaths of fresh air, but her words seem to stir me.

"You need a lock pick."

"I haven't got a bloody lock pick, you idiot."

Of course she hasn't. I try again.

"You need two pieces of wire. A paperclip, a hair grip, something like that."

Bunny's hands reach to her hair. "I've got a hair grip!" she shrieks. "What do I do now?"

I turn and see the flames engulf the wall behind me. The water from the showers is gone, and the smoke is overpowering despite the trickle of fresh air from the window. Panic is rising within me. Each time I cough I feel the terror. I need to force the window. I need to smash it. I need to smash the whole world apart and get out. I drive my shoulder into the wall and it screams in pain, but I don't care. I'll just keep doing it until the world falls apart.

But Bunny is still shouting at me. She is waving the hair grip at me. "Don't give in," she screams. "Please, Archie, don't give in."

I have heard the words before. When I felt the same. When I was fighting and kicking and hitting. When I never wanted to stop. When Dad took the blows and the punches and the anger and just crushed me in his arms, squeezing his limbs around mine and forcing my face into his chest to hide my eyes from the chaos I had caused.

Don't give in, he whispered.

Don't give in, he said.

We can beat it together. You are not on your own.

Let's just go through the routine one more time, he says.

And I open my eyes.

Bunny's eyes are green. Her hair is yellow. Her skin is a kind of a brown and the sky behind her is blue. She is there for me and I am going to get out.

I force the panic out of my mind and start again.

"Snap it in two," I say. "Both pieces will have a slight bend at the end where they were joined. Hold the lock in front of you so you are looking at the bottom of the padlock with the keyhole pointing downwards. Push the piece with the bigger bend at the end into the lock, so the long piece is pointing sideways to the lock and try and turn it to the right."

Bunny is staring at it with terror in her eyes. "It won't turn!" she shouts. "It won't turn!"

"Not yet but keep that pressure on." I stop as a huge burst of coughing racks my body and I feel like I'm drowning in hot ash, but I have beaten the fear and keep calm until it passes.

"Push the second piece into the lock with the bent end pointing upwards while keeping the pressure on the first part of the hair grip."

I can see her. Her face is a mask of concentration. She is chewing her lip, and her chins juts out in determination.

"Now what?" she shouts.

"Tip the end of the second piece down towards you so the bent end is pushing up. Keep the pressure on the first piece. You should feel the pins give and the barrel start to turn."

I don't know if I could have explained it better or if I've got the strength to go through it again but the shriek from Bunny tells me I don't need to.

"It's worked, it's worked," she shouts, and her voice is full of relief.

The lock turns and the bolt of the padlock springs open with a sharp click. Bunny is going mad, screaming as she pulls the lock off. She wrenches open the wire window protector and then the window itself.

I feel the fresh air and find a last burst of energy. I throw myself on to the window ledge and Bunny drags me down to the grass, grabbing my arm and forcing me away, metre after metre, until we are at the hedge when she finally drops me on the ground. I turn and watch as black smoke pours into the sky and the fire rages.

I am black from head to toe. My back is in agony and I can't stop coughing but I am out. I want to lie down and sleep but Bunny doesn't let me. She forces

223

me up again, encouraging me, threatening me and practically carrying me for what seems like forever. Seagulls scream overhead, then mix with sirens and we hobble faster until eventually the sounds fade. We stagger down a slope then stumble across stones that pull at my ankles and drag me down to the ground.

And then the water washes over me.

Bunny pushes me in deeper and the cold bites and wakes me up. She pulls off my shirt and splashes me gently across my back, then touches my face and cleans my eyes. I taste the salt of the water, and watch as the tears pour down her cheeks. We stumble back to the shore.

And then there is nothing.

THURSDAY
4.30 p.m.

I wake up in a strange bed. Under faded green covers in a small, tidy bedroom. There is a wardrobe to the side and neat shelves that hold school books organised into subjects, interspersed with old teddies and stuffed monkeys. At the other end of the room is a small desk under a window with a closed laptop on it, a little cactus in a pot and a jewellery box. Next to the door, a guitar is hanging on a hook beside a narrow chest of drawers. Photographs have been stuck to most of the empty wall space. Some of them show a big man with a shaved head and tattoos over his neck and arms. Others show Bunny at different landmarks around the country and lots of them show Little Tony.

I hear voices coming from somewhere in the house. It is Bunny and I guess her mum, and they are arguing. I can't quite make out the words so I try and sit up but my back flashes in agony. When I swing my legs over the side of the bed, my lungs explode into a fit of coughing and my mouth is filled with thick black mucus that I have to swallow. I'm exhausted. I lie back in the bed and rest.

As I lie still, the voices become clearer.

"Of course it wasn't wrong," Bunny's mum is saying. "I'm just—"

"I didn't know where else to go," Bunny interrupts. "I was scared. He couldn't stop coughing."

"That's why he needs proper treatment. I don't deal with these things. I do general nursing."

"I told you," Bunny says. "I can't take him to hospital without asking him first."

"Yes, you told me," her mum replies angrily. "Because he's wanted by the police. I can't believe after all the years we've had with your dad that you could get mixed up in something like this. You need to walk away."

There is a slight pause, then Bunny's voice is gentler. "No, Mum. Please don't cry. It's not like that. He hasn't done anything. I haven't done anything." Her voice becomes muffled. "I'm just trying to help him because he needs it."

I need to go and stop them arguing so I rise slowly

and sit on the edge of the bed, reaching across to open the door a little. Outside the room is a small landing and Bunny and her mum are downstairs. At the top of the stairs, Little Tony sits with his head resting against the banister. Silently listening.

When my door opens, Little Tony flinches as if he's been caught and we stare at each other in silence until I see him relax. Then he looks back down the empty staircase, shuffling up slightly for me to get past. But instead of going down I sit next to him and lean against the wall. He doesn't say anything. Just watches me with big eyes for a moment before staring back through the banister rails.

Their mum is still talking. "It may seem easy, breaking the law," she says. "It may seem glamorous and like you're hurting nobody, but you'll wreck your life and the lives of the people around you."

Now I can hear the tears flowing and her voice is angry. "You're old enough to make your own decisions now," she says. "I made mistakes, so God knows I can't lecture you, but I don't want you to have the same regrets I do."

As she says the last few words her voice gets louder. Little Tony knows when he has to move and he is up, pulling on my shoulder, urging me away back into Bunny's room. I pull the door shut and sit down heavily on the bed while Little Tony stands at my side and puts his fingers to his lips.

I keep quiet. Bunny's mum calls up the stairs at Little Tony that they have two minutes before they leave and then the voice fades again. But he doesn't move. He just stares at me with a serious look on his face and his green eyes wide open. His fingers twist together anxiously.

"Are you going to prison?" he says nervously.

I shake my head. "I hope not," I say quietly.

"You have to take everything out of your pockets and you sit at the table and there are no toys or anything."

I don't know what to say, so I just nod.

"My daddy lives there but he doesn't like it. He wants to come home." Then he pauses. "Are you going to live here now?"

I shake my head. "No. I live somewhere else," I say. "Near London."

He nods, as if he knows all there is to know about London. "I went there to see the King and the soldiers and the big house he lives in and then we went in the

228

air on the Eye, but that was for a very long time and I don't want to do it again."

He hesitates and looks down. "I don't think you should go to prison," he says. "It makes Mummy cry." Then he turns and leaves the room. A minute later I hear him walking carefully down the stairs and I step out to watch him, staying out of sight as Bunny and her mum walk into the hallway. Mrs Bunting is holding a set of car keys and she reaches down to hold Little Tony's hand.

"We're only trying to do the right thing," Bunny says quietly, but her mum just shakes her head.

"Who in this life doesn't think they're trying to do the right thing?" she says. "He needs to be gone before we get home," she adds.

Then they leave.

I go back into the bedroom and sit on the bed, my head in my hands. After a minute something disturbs my lungs and a horrible cough shudders through my body. Then Bunny appears at the door with a glass of water in one hand and a packet of ibuprofen in the other.

"You're awake," she says, and I nod. We are both

silent for a moment, wondering what to say until eventually she breaks the silence.

"I can't believe I picked that lock," she says, smiling weakly.

I smile, which brings on more coughing and more black phlegm. Bunny winces and moves towards me, but I hold up my hand and wait for the coughing to stop.

"You saved my life," I say.

Her smile wavers a little and she shrugs. "Don't know what came over me. How's your back?"

"Painful. How does it look?"

"Some of it's really nasty, but not too much. You're really lucky you managed to keep wet. My mum put some cream on and you didn't even wake up. You should still get it looked at."

I stand and twist to see my back in the mirror and she is right. There is a wide strip where my skin is dark red below my shoulder blades and a patch about the size of a playing card that is yellow and swollen, but apart from that I seem OK. Except the cough is getting worse. I can hardly move without spluttering.

"I heard your mum talking and she's right. We need to give it all up. I need to hand myself in."

"Yes," she says. "If you tell the police everything they'll have to listen."

There is a hopeful tone to her voice, but she's wrong. "There still isn't any evidence," I say. "They'll say I'm making it all up to try and get my dad off. That woman police officer fixed it all."

"I know," Bunny says. "I heard what she said."

I don't understand. "How can you have heard? You were waiting near the road."

"Yes, but you called me just before they grabbed you. The line stayed open. I had to turn the volume right up, but I could hear."

"Wow." I'm shocked but I guess it doesn't make much difference. "I'm not sure what good it would do," I say. "They would just say you were making it up to help me."

A small smile plays upon Bunny's lips. "I recorded it," she says. "I figured it might be important." She pulls her mobile out of her pocket and now the smile has turned into a wide grin. "It's all here."

I stare at her, wondering if finally things are going our way. "You recorded it?" I repeat. "How did you even think that fast?"

She shrugs modestly, though she can't keep the

smile off her face while she plays the recording. Some parts are hard to hear, but a lot of it is clear and for the first time I think we might have something. Bunny's looking at me and I can feel that energy in my shoulders and suddenly I want to cheer. They are admitting everything and we've got them recorded.

"This should be enough, shouldn't it?" she says. "If we play it to the police, your dad will be in the clear."

"We still need to be careful," I say. "That woman will make sure they don't take two kids seriously. It could take days to get someone to listen. Dad is in danger now."

Bunny thinks for a second, then snaps her fingers. "Why don't you go to the court?" she says. "There will be a judge and barristers and all sorts of people around. Someone will know what to do. Your dad will have a lawyer. He'll be able to help. I've seen how it works. Someone will listen."

A horrible racking cough that seems to drag up half of my lungs bursts out of me but I don't care. I go to fill the glass with water in the bathroom and as I do I stare at myself in the mirror.

"OK," I say. "Tell me how to get back to the house. I'll get an early train. He's in court in the morning so I'll go there and wait for his lawyer."

Bunny shakes her head. "You can't go on your own," she says. "I'll come with you."

"No way. Not after what your mum said."

I stare at her. There is a fierceness in her eyes and her jaw is set. "I promised my mum I wouldn't do anything stupid, dangerous or illegal," she says. "And I'm not going to. Getting you on a train to London isn't any of those things and I'm not leaving it now. Not if it can get those people locked up and help my dad." She clenches her fist. "You can't do it on your own," she adds.

I can't help but grin. "What would I have done without you?" I say, then I hold up my hands. "Don't answer that. Just get me back to the house."

One more day, I say to myself. *I've just got to get through one more day.*

FRIDAY
9.22 a.m.

Most trains from Brighton to London go into Victoria but there are some into St Pancras and we take one of these. I know there will be plain-clothes policemen scattered around the station and when there are no reports of a dead body in the fire they will all be looking for me.

But I've gone through too much to be caught now.

According to the court website, Dad's hearing is scheduled for ten thirty and our train is already twenty minutes late. Bunny and I sit opposite each other, both dressed in smart suits that I hope will make us look older, and I am wearing an old pair of sunglasses. We lean forward with our elbows on the table between us so we can whisper to each other, but for now there is nothing to say as we wait for the doors to open. I remind myself to try and look like an office worker who belongs here with all the others, then take one last deep breath as the people around us stand up to depart. Finally we get off the train.

It feels like every pair of eyes is on us as we make our way through the barriers towards the underground then stop to look at the Tube map. As Bunny checks the route on her phone against the map, I notice a police officer standing at the entrance to the Tube and another one by the small convenience store to the side. Crouching to tie my shoelace, I see several more, standing in all directions, scanning the station concourse. They are everywhere, and panic grips me. I need to get out of here now, so I stand with my head bowed and grab Bunny by the elbow, guiding her forward. But before we get far, another officer steps right in front of us. He is talking on his radio only a few metres away and I can almost feel his eyes settle on me. I see his eyes narrow slightly as he takes me in, before I feel Bunny's arm jerk out of my grip.

"Go," she whispers, and before I can react she darts to the convenience store and grabs a handful of chocolate. The store owner yells and all eyes turn, including the police officer's, as Bunny stands with the chocolate in her hand then seems to notice the officer for the first time, staring at him for a moment while the shopkeeper is still screaming that she's a thief. Her eyes turn to meet mine for an instant and she nods once.

Then she drops the chocolate and runs.

The police officer's first reaction is to take off after her but she is at the main doors within a few seconds, then out into the sunshine. He follows, yelling to two more officers by the doors, who rush to help, while I put my head down and march towards the underground. Except, as I do, the first officer stops suddenly and turns back towards me, just as I start down the escalator.

He shouts at me to stop, then leaves the other officers to follow Bunny while he sprints after me, so I speed up, barging my way through commuters, ignoring their angry protests and the burning in my lungs. I can't run for long and already I can feel the coughing bursting out of me, but I force myself through the crowd until I reach a barrier that leads to the Victoria Line. A woman in front of me puts her ticket in the machine and I shove my way through with her, forcing us both hard through the turnstile. I hear the police officer behind, screaming for people to get out of the way and calling for back-up on his radio but I am in London and people are not helpful.

They get in his way and buy me a few extra seconds.

I am coughing as I run but I am not going to give up. I duck through the small passageway to the southbound platform of the Victoria Line where a crammed row of people stand, waiting for the train. The board above their heads says the next one is approaching so I push between two women then dart along the platform edge, keeping the line of people between me and the police officer until I hear whistling from the tunnel behind me, followed by a roar as the train rushes into the station. The doors open as I reach the end of the platform. And I step up on to the train.

People jostle each other as they get on and off and I rip off my jacket in the confusion, then turn and stare as the officer runs out on to the platform at the other end of the train. He can't be sure I'm here but I feel his eyes searching and every fibre in my body is praying he stays in the station, but he doesn't. As the doors close, he waits until the last second and gets on the train. I can feel myself sweating as I check the time. Dad's case is due to be heard in about half an hour.

I can't afford to be late.

I need to get changed and fast, but there is nowhere out of sight so I push my way through the passengers as the train starts, moving to the wider space where the carriages join. Then I stop and crouch down to face the carriage side, opening my bag in front of me as if looking in it while I untie my shoelaces and undo my trousers. Then in one movement I stand and step out of my shoes and trousers, leaving them bunched on the floor in front of me so now I am wearing the bright-blue shorts I had on beneath. In another moment I stoop to pick up the abandoned clothes and shove my feet into the beach shoes I had taken from my bag, before marching further down the carriage, unbuttoning my shirt as I go. As I twist between other passengers, I pull my arms from my sleeves and rip the smart shirt and tie off to reveal my bright-red T-shirt. Stepping through the next set of seats, I shove the smart clothes into my black bag and switch everything into the bright-orange shopping bag that was folded in my rucksack pocket. It has taken around twenty seconds. And nobody has looked up from their screens.

I keep going, pulling on a cap and swapping my pair of clear-lens glasses for the sunglasses as I enter another carriage, staggering as a burst of coughing almost forces me to collapse. I lean against the stained wall of the carriage, forcing my breathing to calm and wondering how much longer I can go on. Every part of my body aches, and it seems like it's only adrenalin that's keeping me going. Finally I move forward again and enter the middle carriage of the train. At exactly the same time as the police officer.

I freeze and think about turning but I can't run again and he can't be sure I'm on the train so I take my chances. There's an empty seat between a sprawled young guy wearing headphones and a suited businessman so I squeeze myself into it, picking up one of the free newspapers that litters the seats and staring at it with blank eyes. The beat of my neighbour's music pounds like my heart and I cover my mouth and try not to cough, sensing when the policeman reaches me and staring at his black boots under the paper. *Just keep walking*, I urge in my mind. But he doesn't. He stops in front of me.

"Excuse me." His voice is gruff and hurried and I know I have made the wrong decision. There is nowhere to run and I should have stayed at the back of the train.

"Excuse me," he repeats.

I watch as his hand reaches down through my line of vision and wait for the contact on my shoulder but it doesn't come. And then the man next to me shuffles upright, scowling and pulling back his sprawled legs, which are blocking the space between the seats and preventing the policeman from getting through. The officer goes past, and the man stretches out again. And I keep perfectly still.

He goes through into the next carriage and I get up, feeling the train slow as we pull into Warren Street station. People stand, moving towards the door, and I move with them. The doors open and I get off the train, staying in the mill of people making their way towards the illuminated signs to the Northern Line. As I turn a corner I start to jog and then to run, and no one follows me. Within a minute I am southbound, changing at Leicester Square to the Piccadilly Line, then again at Holborn on to the Central Line to go to St Paul's to get to the Old Bailey. I look at my phone again and now it is twelve minutes past ten.

I am running out of time.

FRIDAY
10.16 a.m.

My phone buzzes as soon as I step into the bright sunshine at St Paul's. It's a voicemail from Bunny and I clamp my phone to my ear, desperate to check if she is OK.

"It's me," she says. "Are you OK? I got changed in McDonald's and lost them. Let me know you're OK," she repeats. "I'm going to get a Tube so if I'm underground leave a message."

I can hear her panting as she runs, then she speaks again.

"Something else," she says. "I called Dad to leave a message about what's going on and he answered. They've let him out!" Excitement bursts through her voice. "We couldn't talk long because he had paperwork to do but he's been released."

I can hear her relief as she speaks. "He said your dad came good for him, although he didn't say how. But let me know you're all right. And good luck."

I try her number but get voicemail, so I leave a message as I turn the corner on to Holborn Viaduct and head towards the Old Bailey. The road is busy with cars. Petrol fumes shimmer in the heat and my skin feels dirty almost immediately in the London air. My back is hurting and my mouth feels black, but I don't slow down. I just hurry on.

Then I see the courts. Above me, gleaming in the sunshine and marking the way, is the Statue of Justice, shining like gold with her arms stretched out, holding the sword and the scales. I follow her direction to the Old Bailey but I don't turn into it, just look carefully as I cross the road, taking in the few people milling about in the quiet street. A dark-suited lawyer with a large briefcase turns into the main entrance where he is greeted by a security guard. A woman stands next to the court lists, talking on her mobile phone while two men with cameras talk idly to each other, but otherwise the street is empty.

I reach the other side, then continue on for around fifty metres before turning and coming down the road again. As I watch, two yellow-jacketed police officers emerge from the entrance and I quicken my pace, raising my phone to the side of my face as I go past. The woman has finished her call and walks up to them to go in and I hear them asking her for photo identification. They explain that they have been asked to check all visitors today and I feel gripped with nerves. I don't know what I was expecting, I need to find another way in.

I keep walking and turn right into Warwick Lane, which opens into a square, and now I can see the concrete rear of the Central Criminal Court. About five paces in front of that there is a high metal railing and then a grass bank keeping people out. To my left there is an entrance to a small brick passageway where a group of students are milling around.

I walk through the middle of the group down a number of steps into a tiled Victorian tunnel. Ahead of me on the wall is a large sign indicating the entrance to the public gallery and a list of rules next to a heavy metal door on the right. No cameras, no bags, no phones, no recording devices, no one under fourteen. I watch as a couple approach the door, dressed smartly and holding hands nervously, and I wonder if they are the family of a defendant. The door opens and the couple go inside, but again they are met by a police officer and a security guard who wait until they produce ID.

I tell myself to be patient, that I will find the way, but now I am starting to panic. I retrace my steps through the passage towards the rear of the block. On the far side of the square there is another entrance through a wide iron gate with an entryphone on the side and a camera directed at it. Through the gate I can see a small courtyard filled with expensive cars, which I guess is where the judges park, but again I can't see any way in. I look at my phone again as my heart pounds and the coughing seizes my body. It is twenty-five past ten and time is running out.

Frantically I scan the building again, talking to myself as the panic rises. Dad is in there and I feel like I am on my own.

"I don't know what to do," I mutter to myself. "I don't know what to do." I run back down to the tunnel but I am going nowhere and just moving for the sake of it. I go back to the railings and grip the bars with my hands and now I am almost shouting. "Come on, Dad," I say. "I'm trying to be patient but I don't know what to do!"

A woman turns to look at me quizzically. She has a friendly smile and she is wearing a blue dress with flowers on it like one Mum used to have. She catches my eye then turns away and suddenly I can hear Mum's voice echo through my mind as if she is standing next to me. *Being patient is all very well,* she whispers, *but sometimes you have to just close your eyes and jump.*

And I am back there again, on that sunny day when we were having a picnic in the country. When the world seemed big and Mum wanted to cross this small stream but Dad wouldn't agree on the right place. They were arguing but holding hands and I couldn't quite understand why if they were arguing. Mum was telling Dad how frustrated she was getting, but she was laughing at the same time until she'd just had enough. She grabbed my hand and she ran at the stream, charged at it full speed so we had to jump and soar before we landed on the other side in a kind of stunned silence that just poured back into laughter.

I miss her now like I can't breathe. I miss her like you just have to touch the world to see it smash because there's nothing holding it together. And I'm standing there outside that courtroom and suddenly I realise how much I miss him too because we used to be together in every way but now all we have is race night. So I can't give up, I've got to find a way in. And I'm going to just jump.

Sometimes you just have to risk everything, she said. And I know she was right.

Some windows on the first floor are open because of the heat, and net curtains flutter in and out, carried on the breeze from fans inside. All the windows are barred but there is one above the entrance to the car park, where the bars look just wide enough for me to get through. It's my only chance.

Ignoring the CCTV cameras, I grab hold of the railings, then use every ounce of strength that I've got to swing myself up until I am balanced on the top. I crouch down and get my feet on to the flat part of the rails while holding on to the tops of the iron posts, then shuffle to the end of the fence that is against the wall of the building above the entryphone. Then I stand up.

And I jump.

The cameras will have spotted me by now and the students are staring but I don't care. My left hand hits a bar, hard, and a jolt of pain fires in my arm. My fingers slip and I swing into the windowsill, but my right hand clenches around the cold white iron and

I hold on desperately. I swing myself back, hauling myself up with my right hand then grabbing the bars with my left, ignoring whatever's in the room and sliding my legs through the bars. My feet tangle in the net curtains then hit something inside. Somebody cries out and I wait for hands to grab me but they don't come.

I raise my arms over my head like a diver, then twist until I can squeeze my shoulders through. My feet slide, perhaps on paper, and my hips land on something. I lower my arms and now only my head is outside, but it seems too big to get between the bars. In a last desperate surge, I pull my head through. There is a flash of pain as I feel like my left ear is being ripped off and I tumble into the room.

I crash hard on to a desk in front of the window, kicking a computer screen to the floor, where it smashes. My legs sprawl over the desk but there is not enough room and I tip backwards on to the floor, landing on my back and spilling paper all around. My back explodes in pain but I ignore it and force myself up again. Then I look around the room.

It is an office with two desks. Behind the other desk a woman is standing, her hand over her mouth, staring at me. When I meet her gaze, she seems to jolt out of her shock and turns towards the door with a scream on her lips. But I beat her to it. I dash to the door and race through it, bursting out into the passageway.

I hear the scream behind me as I rush down the narrow, empty corridor. The carpet is bright blue and old-fashioned, and the walls are a plain sombre green. Some of the doors on either side of me begin to open in response to the noise, but I ignore them and carry on until I reach a crossroads next to a staircase. A man shouts at me to stop, but I ignore him too and he looks too confused to follow.

There are signs on the wall and the online court lists said court sixteen so I frantically search for it before racing down the stairs. Above me, I hear the heavy tramp of feet and a voice calling into a radio about an intruder as the whole building seems to explode into activity. I reach the door to court sixteen as the clock above it ticks through to ten thirty-five.

I shove the door open and burst in.

FRIDAY
10.35 a.m.

I am in a large courtroom that is mostly empty. At the front, a woman dressed in formal robes and a wig is sitting in a high-backed green leather chair stamped with the royal crest. In front of her is a row of four chairs with two administrators, who appear to be taking notes. In front of them are four long tables with green office chairs where two barristers are sitting, also wearing wigs. To the judge's right are two tiers of seats and long desks with a set of steps up the middle, but there is no jury and no one in them. On the left-hand side of the court is an empty witness box and above that the public gallery where a few students are sitting.

And at the back of the court, encased in clear security-strength Perspex, is my dad.

When he sees me, he leaps to his feet and starts hammering on the plastic in front of him.

"Archie!" he shouts. "Archie!"

There is a guard on each side of him but I ignore them and run up to the dock. "I've worked it out, Dad!" I shout back. "I've worked it out."

I look at him for a moment and I notice the grey in his hair and the lines on his face. He stares at me, fear and shock in his eyes, but maybe hope too. He looks OK and I'm so relieved to see that he hasn't been hurt that I almost stop. I reach out to touch the Perspex but it is cold and hard and then everyone starts shouting at once so I keep moving.

More guards rush in behind me, blocking the exits, and there is no space left to run so I jump on to the table in front of me and bound from desk to desk until I reach the front. Everyone is on their feet now, yelling and backing away, but I ignore them and shout as loud as I can over all the noise.

"Stop the case, my dad's innocent. I've got proof. You've got to stop the hearing."

I fling myself over the last table and suddenly I am next to the judge. "You've got to stop the hearing," I say desperately. "I've got proof he's innocent. I know who did it. You've got to let my dad go."

But instead of listening, the judge jerks up and backs away. An armed police officer dives in front of

250

her and reaches for his weapon. Hands grab me from behind and I thrash against them, but they bundle me to the ground and someone rams a knee into my back. My hands are pulled behind me and a hand forces my face into the floor so I can't speak. Someone shouts, "Safe," and slowly the room calms. I am staring at the judge, who is breathing hard and looking relieved. She nods at the security guard, who pulls me roughly to my feet and bundles me towards the door.

But at the last minute she changes her mind.

"Wait, please," she says, staring right at me. "Are you Archie Blake?"

I turn to look at her, ignoring the pain as I struggle against the security guard's firm grip, trying to read her expression.

"Yes."

The judge looks to the back of the court.

"This is your son?"

Dad's voice is hoarse when he speaks. "Yes, Your Honour."

The judge looks back to me. "You're the one that's been missing," she says. "Where have you been?"

"In Brighton, Your Honour. I was trying to find out what was going on. Now I know and I can prove it."

"And how can you do that?"

"I know who's behind it all. It's another police officer. I don't know her name, but I know what she looks like. And I know how it all works."

"That's not proof."

"No, Your Honour, but I've got a recording of her admitting it all on my phone. I can play it for you."

The judge nods slowly, her eyes still fixed on mine. The guard releases my hands and I take out my phone and open the app. I am about to press play when there is a movement behind me and suddenly the phone is ripped from my hand.

"Your Honour, my name is Superintendent Lisa Mackenzie. Let me take this boy away. If he's got evidence we'll look at it."

I recognise the voice first, and when I turn to see her face there is fire in her dark eyes. I reel away in horror, but she grabs my arm, twisting it behind my back, practically breaking it and making me cry out in pain. She knows I recognise her and she is pulling me away, moving forcefully, talking all the time. "There's no need to delay things any longer, Your Honour," she says. "We'll get to the bottom of it."

I scream out, ignoring the pain in my arm. "It's her!"

I shout. "It's her!" But I can't escape from her grip. She grabs the phone in her other hand and marches me towards the exit, pulling me away from the judge's bench as the court rises in confusion. I struggle but the pain is so much I practically collapse. Then the two security guards take over, seizing an arm each and marching me towards the door.

Dad is staring at Mackenzie with a stunned expression on his face. His hand flies to his open mouth and I see the blood drain from his cheeks while his eyes fill with rage. He shouts something out about trust but the words are hard to hear as everyone in the court is shouting too. I notice a tear rolling down his cheek but then I am hauled away as the doors open behind me and one of the guards drags me through into the corridor behind.

Then everything stops as the judge's voice booms out, freezing the movement and silencing the court.

"Wait!" she says. "I want to hear what he has to say."

"But, Your Honour—" Mackenzie starts, but she is cut off.

"I want to hear what he has to say," the judge says firmly, "and then I will make up my own mind."

I feel the grip on my arms loosen and I am dragged back into the court. I stare at Mackenzie, seeing the fear in her eyes as she desperately tries to think of a way out. She tries to argue but the judge calls me forward.

"I am Judge Swelling," she says. "Presiding over this bail hearing. Are you really accusing this officer?"

Now the moment is here I don't know where to start. I stare at her. "My dad's innocent," I say. "This woman set him up. She's going to kill him. She killed my mum. She tried to kill me yesterday."

Mackenzie interrupts. "Your Honour, this is nonsense," she laughs, but the laugh is forced. "I was in London all weekend working on another case."

"Rubbish," I snap. "She was in Brighton. She tried to kill me." And then I remember. "I've got the diamonds," I shout, ripping the necklace out of my pocket and throwing it down on the table. "And I've got proof. Let me play it to you, please."

I watch and it feels like time has stopped while Swelling picks up the necklace and examines it. Mackenzie is tense next to me but she doesn't speak. The judge looks from one stone to another and I feel dread rush into the pit of my stomach. She has to listen, doesn't she? After all we've been through, she has to listen to me.

Then, finally, the judge's gaze moves from the diamonds to me and our eyes meet. She nods slowly.

"Let's hear it then."

I reach out and grab the phone in Mackenzie's hand. For a moment, she doesn't let go and our eyes lock together. I hold her gaze, seeing her fear turn slowly into hatred as I rip the phone free and hold it out. But then my hopes crash again.

There is something wrong and the phone won't work. Mackenzie must have hit it against one of the desks or something because there is a big crack down the front so the screen won't respond. I look up at the judge in horror.

"She's broken it." I hold the phone to show her but before she can speak, Mackenzie speaks, looking at the judge earnestly, holding her hands out before her as if to prove her honesty.

"Your Honour, we don't know what pressure this young man has been under but, really, I'm not sure this is the time. We should not lose sight of the fact that this boy has been brought up for the last few years by the man who is in your dock accused of a number of crimes." She gestures at Dad and I feel the panic rising inside me.

She carries on. "It is sad but perhaps not surprising that the boy has got a mixed-up view of things and accuses the first officer he sees. Shouldn't we go through things one step at a time, starting with today's bail hearing?"

The judge is still holding the diamonds but she puts them down, taking off her wig and running her hands over her face. She looks at me, then seems to make a decision.

"I'm sorry, Archie, we have to follow the appropriate procedure. Without this proof of yours we can't continue."

She hesitates and I am about to speak but she holds up her hands, her voice firm and determined. "You can't just throw around accusations. You will be taken to make a statement while we get on with things here. I'm sure you will be looked after."

My eyes meet Mackenzie's and I see the triumph in her cold, dark gaze. One of the guards takes my arm and Mackenzie takes the other, clamping her hand over my mouth. At the back of the room I see Dad shouting and being restrained. Slowly, the room goes quiet and I am dragged to the exit.

And then the voice rings out.

"*I killed your mother, I framed your father, and now I'm going to kill you.*"

A pulse seems to fire through the court. The words repeat. Over and over again. Mackenzie's voice, recorded, muffled and overamplified, is playing from the phone in Bunny's hand as she leans over the balcony of the public gallery. But it is enough. Gradually the court goes quiet to hear. And the words become clear.

Mackenzie spins around in panic. "Turn that off!" she shouts. "Turn those lies off now."

But Bunny doesn't. Sensing the judge's eyes upon her, Bunny holds out the phone as far as she can to try and make the sound louder.

"It's true," she shouts. "I'm a witness. She tried to kill Archie in a fire. It was her."

Her finger stretches out towards Mackenzie and everyone's eyes follow it. For a moment, Mackenzie hesitates. Words form on her lips. She starts to speak then stops, turning and backing towards the door. Then she runs.

She shoves me away from her and springs towards

the door to the court, throwing it open and bursting into the corridor. I crash hard into a bench, then pull myself to my feet and within seconds I'm chasing after her.

Mackenzie holds out her badge, calling for the crowds to make way for police. I am around twenty metres behind but catching up as she is slowed by the people who can't get out of the way fast enough. She barges into a man, causing the papers he is carrying to fly up in the air, then she forces open a fire door and runs outside. I slow to weave past him then burst out into the light.

Mackenzie is running hard but I keep going after her. I turn into a busy street, dodging between pedestrians until I reach a large bridge that runs over the river. Mackenzie turns and stares at me, then ducks into an underpass. I can hear sirens now, getting louder, but I am still the only one chasing. I turn down the underpass, but Mackenzie is waiting.

She grabs me and shoves me forcefully against the concrete of the embankment barrier. I squint in the sudden gloom as her face presses close to mine. Her fear and the vulnerability are gone. All that's left is anger.

"You've ruined everything," she hisses, traces of spittle flecking her lips. "My plans – you've ruined them all."

"You killed my mother!" I hurl back. "You deserve to go to prison forever."

She slams me hard against the barrier, knocking the air out of me, and my back explodes in agony. I throw a punch but Mackenzie blocks it and starts dragging me up on to the barrier towards the river.

Then a policeman turns around the corner, screaming at Mackenzie to release me. She hesitates. Her grip is still firmly on my shirt, but her eyes dart over to him for a moment. She turns and I can see a kind of madness raging in her stare. She lowers her face until it is a centimetre from mine.

"I'll come back for you. This isn't finished. One day we'll be even."

She releases me, shifting her weight to escape, but I refuse to let go. With one last effort, I wrap my arms around her waist and throw her backwards. For a moment we are both balanced on the lip of the barrier, locked together, pushing frantically against each other, and then we lurch back. I stick out my arm, scraping my fingers against the cold concrete to stop myself falling, but Mackenzie can't hold on. There is nothing I can do to stop her. She tumbles into the water.

My arm is screaming with pain but I cling on desperately until the policeman reaches me to pull me back and lay me on the ground. He tells me to stay still and I hear him radioing for an ambulance and a river team. A second officer arrives and kneels down to check my injuries but I push him away and drag myself up to the barrier to look over.

There is nothing. No movement in the water, no splashing and no sign of Mackenzie at all.

I can feel the officer's hands on my shoulders and I let him pull me to the ground. He tells me to rest and I don't argue. My back is on fire, my arm is in agony and my lungs feel like they are going to burst. I close my eyes for a moment, then find I don't want to open them again.

I just lie still and let unconsciousness swallow me up.

FRIDAY
4.07 p.m.

I open my eyes, then close them. After another minute or so I open them again. There is a moment of nothingness when I am half awake before I come to, then my vision clears and I focus on the sights and sounds of the room.

I am lying on my front, my head turned to my right. There is a small mask over my face releasing something cool and clear and wonderful into my lungs. My hands are palm down on either side of my head and I can see bruises along my right forearm where I hit it falling from the desk to the floor. The sheets and pillowcase are white and the wall in front of me is a blank grey. There are shadow patterns fluttering on the wall as the curtains behind me dance in a slight breeze. Somewhere else I can hear muted sounds of movement but it doesn't disturb me. There is something cold that feels soothing pressed against my back.

After a few more moments of stillness, a dull pain swells in my head and I feel thirsty. I lift my head to turn to face into the room. As I do, the mask twists and I have a brief moment of dizziness. Pain flashes behind my eyes and I struggle slightly with the tube, until an arm reaches across and helps me untangle it so I can turn over. I blink groggily and pull the mask roughly away from my face, before finally turning my head and slumping back down on to the pillow. I feel exhausted. Any energy I had is gone and pain seems to spread through every part of my body. I close my eyes and breathe deeply, but I am still thirsty so I open them again.

And then it doesn't matter any more. Because Dad is sitting next to me and he is smiling.

Our eyes meet and he leans forward to smooth the sheet across my back. "Hey, Archie," he says. "You've finally woken up then."

I can't think of anything to say. There is too much to talk about and nowhere to start.

"I worked it out," I manage, and maybe it's enough.

"I know you did. Your friend Bunny told me."

"Is she OK?"

"She's fine. She wants to see you, but they said you

needed to rest. She's with her dad."

There is a pause before I ask the question I'm dreading. "Are you free now?" I say. "Is it all over?"

Dad shifts uncomfortably in his chair. "I think so..." he says, then hesitates. "There's still an investigation to be held, but I've been released. After Mackenzie ran off it was obvious to everyone that she was guilty of something and that cast a lot of doubt over the evidence they had against me. My lawyer asked the judge to dismiss the charges until there was an investigation and she agreed."

"Did they catch her?"

"No." Dad utters the single syllable bluntly. "We don't know where she is. They swept the river but didn't find a body." Then he looks away again. "But maybe it's for the best."

"Because without her they can't prove you did anything?"

He looks at me, and there is guilt in his eyes. "You wanted to catch them, didn't you, Dad?" I say. "Did she trick you into stealing the necklace?"

Dad looks down. "Sort of," he says. "She said the name Taylor gave me was a dead end and when my application for a search warrant was rejected, I lost patience. I had this crazy thought that Mum's killers would still want the necklace and I thought I could use it to get to them. But it was a stupid thing to do."

"I think we need to leave it alone now," I say. "Mum would hate it all. I think it's time to feel normal again."

He looks at me and there is a tear in his eye. "I think you're right," he says. "You and me. Let's make it work."

I lie back for a moment and feel the tension fade away. Dad helps me take a drink from the glass then fills it up again.

"Did they catch the others?" I ask.

"Brighton Police have made several arrests. Someone called Radcliffe wants to do a deal. It looks like we'll get them all."

"That's great."

Dad has a sip of the water. "Do you want to rest now?" he says.

"I'm OK to keep talking," I say. "I'm glad you're here."

"It's been a long week. I can't believe what you've been through."

I look away. "I did some bad things too."

"I know. It's OK."

"What did you do for Taylor?"

"Only what was right," he says, and this time there

is no doubt in his eyes. "He was determined to go straight. He just needed someone on his side."

I lean back and stare at the ceiling. "It's easy to break the law, isn't it?"

"Only takes one moment," he says. "But it can take a long time to put things right."

I smile. "There's some dry cleaning I need to take back."

"I'll sort it."

There is a pause, then I look back at Dad. "When we were mucking around, when it was race night," I say, "did you ever think that stuff would come in useful?"

Dad laughs quietly. "No," he says. "But I guess it was a bit, wasn't it?" He shrugs. "How would you fancy a new start? The two of us. Away from London and all this."

As soon as he says it, I know it is the right thing to do. I ask him where and he suggests Brighton, and I wonder if he's been thinking about it for more than just the last minute.

"I think that would be great," I say. I can't think of anything that I want more.

I'm feeling tired again and my eyes are heavy. I want to keep talking but I don't think I can stay awake. I can feel Dad's hand on my hair as he strokes it like Mum used to and I hear his words as I drift off.

"I'm proud of you," he says. "We'll make it together. Just like Mum would want us to."

I close my eyes and sleep peacefully.

MONDAY
11.36 a.m.

The rough voice crashes through the corridor and I am up and out of the chair as fast as I can remember moving.

"I keep telling you. He needs to see me. Now, which room is he in?"

Bunny sticks her head around the door then rushes in and practically crushes me in her arms. I cry out in pain as a nurse appears behind her looking concerned, but I hold my hands up to him and tell him it's OK.

"It's all right," I gasp. "She's my friend."

"Visiting hours aren't until two," the nurse says. "She should come back then."

But I shake my head. "I'm leaving now," I say. "She's come to collect me. My dad's just getting the car."

The nurse goes and I sit back down on the bed, breathing heavily. Bunny looks at me and grins.

"Stop whining," she says. "You're all sorted. Your dad said you were OK to come home."

"I still need some rest," I say defensively. "My back will need another week for the blistering to heal. I've sprained my shoulder, broken a rib and practically ripped off my ear. Oh yeah, and it will take a month or two for my lungs to get over breathing in all that smoke."

She laughs. "But apart from that you're fine, right?"

"Never better," I say, laughing too. "Are you OK?"

She walks across to the window and dumps her bag on the chair in front of it. "I'm fine," she says. "I'm a lot tougher than you are. And I've got something to show you."

She reaches into her bag and pulls out a copy of *The Times*. "I didn't know if you'd seen it. You're famous. Page seven."

I take the paper and open it, as a sense of anxiety rises inside me. I turn to page seven and stop when I see the headline.

Thirteen-year-old boy exposes police corruption

Thirteen-year-old Archie Blake was recovering in hospital yesterday after exposing a complex plot involving a corrupt police officer and the theft of a £5-million diamond necklace...

I read on and the memories flood back through my mind. The mad escape in the night, the pain in all my muscles as I clung to the table in the jeweller's, the terror as I watched the smoke drifting into the pavilion. I shake my head and try to clear them away.

Bunny leans over my shoulder. "It's mostly rubbish anyway," she says. "There's no mention of all the bad stuff you had to do. And there's no mention of me either, which is worse."

I laugh. "What did Dad think of it?"

Bunny's face turns serious. "He was furious. Said the two of you should just be left alone."

"He was talking about leaving London," I say. "Starting again somewhere."

"Because Mackenzie knows where you live?"

"Maybe. She still hasn't shown up then?"

Bunny shakes her head. "She's legged it. The police think she's gone abroad." She stops suddenly and stares at me. "I'm sorry, Archie," she says. "I'm sure it'll be all right. She won't come back."

Maybe it doesn't matter if she does or doesn't. "Give us a chance to catch her and lock her up," I say.

"Any idea where you'll move to?"

"Apparently there's a nice little semi in Rottingdean

269

going spare. Lousy neighbours, but a nice area."

She stares at me with her mouth open. "You are kidding, right?"

I shake my head, trying to stop the grin taking over my face.

"Actually," she says, "I think you'll find the neighbours are just about to get a bit friendlier."

"Now your dad's out, you mean?"

But she shakes her head. "My mum's getting married. They said they'd love to have me stay but I think she'd like some space. And Dad asked me to move in with him."

"What's your dad like?"

Bunny laughs. "You wait till you meet him. You won't know what hit you."

She's got a smile on her face that means she's not going to give me any more so I don't press it. I stand up and Bunny takes my bag for me. "We'd better get down to reception," I say. "Dad'll be waiting."

We're standing together in the lift when I notice Bunny watching me in the mirror. She looks thoughtful, like she's trying to work something out, but when I ask, she just shakes her head and tells me it's nothing. Then we reach the ground floor and I can see Dad across the reception by the entrance. I wave and start to walk on, until Bunny's hand on my arm stops me.

"You know," she says in a quiet voice, "I still don't understand why your dad taught you all that stuff."

She's being so serious I don't quite get it. "What do you mean?" I say.

"The lock-picking and the safe-opening and all that. Why would he show you how to do it? What was it all for?"

I look across at Dad, then back at her. "I told you," I say. "It was just a way of us doing things together after Mum died. He said that when we were like that, we could forget she wasn't with us." I shrug and smile.

She smiles back. "I guess you're right." She winks at me. "Just a shame you'll never get to use any of it again, isn't it?"

I frown for a moment, then start to walk on. "I guess it is," I say, as she jogs to catch up. "Although you never know, do you?" I whisper to myself. "And tonight is race night."

Acknowledgements

Thanks to Ludo and Eve for spotting this and seeing something good in it. Thanks to Tom for making it happen. Special thanks to Naomi and Poppy for reading every version because this book was a long time coming (and there were a lot of drafts). And especially to Ben who convinced me that ten-year-old boys would think that being brilliant at stealing stuff was cool. Only in fiction, obviously. Never in the real world. Honest. I promise!

LOOK OUT FOR THIS ACTION-PACKED THRILLER, ALSO BY SIMON FOX

Turn over for a sneak peek...

1

NOW

I can steal time.

The most I can take at the moment is fifteen seconds, which is not a lot. Grandmother took almost three minutes once and she told me she's done more, but I never saw it. And when she was tired, which was more and more often, or pretending not to be sad, which was pretty much always, she struggled to get to half that.

She says there are stories of someone who can take all the time in the world, but how can that be right? She said it when she was trying to get me to concentrate, when she was urging me to focus. As if all I had to do was understand what was possible to make it happen. It sounded unbelievable but when she said it there was a kind of memory in her eyes and something about her look that made me think maybe it was more than just a wild story.

And we didn't need all the time in the world, did we? We just needed enough to get to England. To fight and crash and tear our way to England where Dad said we would be safe. I hoped a few seconds might be enough to keep the two of us from getting caught but I guess I was wrong. We started with everything and I ended with nothing. On a beach in the dark; cold wet and empty.

I should have practised more. Because every second is precious. And I never took enough.

2

AFTER

He grabs my collar and hauls me up the beach. There is anger in his grip and fear on his face, reflected yellow in the strange lamps that light the seafront path. He half runs and now he lets go, but I don't stop. Stones shift under my feet and my wet jeans rub hard against my legs but I don't slow down. We reach the tarmac and he swerves to the right, twisting briefly to check I am still there.

"Keep up," he says. But he doesn't need to.

I turn, briefly, as we hurry forward. Blue lights flash into the black sky and shouts rebound against the crash of the waves, behind the sounds of our hard breathing and the slap of our feet against the road. We run with the cliff to our left. Out in front is a deserted cafe, then a pool of light as the path turns up and away from the sea. There is a metal barrier to stop cyclists, then a pub car park, deserted except for a van and two large waste bins.

And three police cars parked in a line like crooked teeth.

Ronnie lurches towards the cliff, gripping my arm and hauling me into some scrubby bushes hidden by the shadow. He curses, hard, under his breath then lies still, panting. I lie next to him, under the rough leaves, close enough to feel the heat of his body, staring up into the light. He takes a phone out his pocket and makes a call, whispering quickly to whoever answers.

"They're everywhere. Did you get out? How many were taken?"

He freezes as two policemen walk quickly past us back to the beach. Then he lies still.

"How many?" I whisper.

"You speak English?" He sounds surprised.

"Yeah. How many?"

"All of them," he says.

I feel the wave of fear rushing through me. Ice burns in my stomach. Panic fills my mind.

"What do we do?"

"We get out of here."

"What about my dad?" I whisper.

"We get out of here," he says again. "Then we find out."

We watch the policemen disappear into the blur of the lights under the cliff then turn back to the way ahead.

"OK. When I say run, we run," Ronnie says. "As fast as you can. Past the cars then up that road. There is a church. Turn left and look for a black BMW. A friend of mine is waiting and will drive us away."

"Is that your plan?" I ask.

He nods then braces himself to move. I put my hand on his arm to stop him.

"That's a terrible plan," I hiss. "You want to get caught?"

He stares at me, surprise and a hint of anger in his eyes. I feel his body tense again as he readies himself to run, but I lean across and push him down flat.

"What do you know about getting caught?" he hisses. "You are just a foreign kid to them. It's all good if they catch you. I am a man. I have a life here. It's different for me."

"So what?" I whisper. "I'll come up with a plan that isn't terrible. Just let me think."

I calm my breathing and still my thoughts like

she showed me. I concentrate on doing nothing, filling my mind with my own image, lying still in the undergrowth. I am doing nothing while the world turns around me. I am locked in place.

I creep forward until I can hear voices and the buzz of radios. Somewhere, a phone goes off, but I ignore it and crawl to the edge of the light. And then I burst out, running as fast as I can, like the winds of hell are on my back. I make it to the cars before the police react, then I swerve to the left. A woman officer stares at me, then yells, and all the heads turn at once. I duck to the left, swerving round with my hand on a car bonnet, pushing shut the car door before the man can get out. I accelerate into the street Ronnie showed me, ignoring the shouts, ignoring the threats, ignoring the burning in my muscles as I tear up the road.

Until a man crashes into my legs and we tumble over. I try to scramble free but he has me tight. Another officer arrives and yanks my hands hard behind my back. I feel metal round my wrists then they haul me to my feet.

I roll on to my back and stare into the darkness.

"We can't do it your way," I hiss. "It won't work."

Ronnie is nervous. He wants to run, but it is the wrong thing to do. "Trust me," I say. "The police will have you in less than fifteen seconds. Wait here," I insist. "They may go in a minute."

They won't go in a minute, but it is what I need to say to stop him running. I look again at the cars. There were two officers in the car on the left, another behind it and the last two standing between the cars. So there is more space to the right. I calm myself again and concentrate, waiting until my heart is still. I am locked in place.

I creep forward until I can hear voices and the buzz of radios. Somewhere, a phone goes off, but I ignore it and crawl to the edge of the light. And then I burst out, running as fast as I can, like the winds of hell are on my back. I make it to the cars before the police react, then swerve to the right. A woman officer turns, moving instinctively but then hesitating, because her view is blocked by the other cars. Then she yells and all the heads turn at once. I race round the right-hand car, leaning on the bonnet, then accelerating away. I hear the slam of a door from the other side, then shouts behind me and footsteps as they give chase.

out, running as fast as I can, like the winds of hell are on my back. I make it to the cars before the police react, then I swerve to the left. A woman officer stares at me, then yells, and all the heads turn at once. I duck to the left, swerving round with my hand on a car bonnet, pushing shut the car door before the man can get out. I accelerate into the street Ronnie showed me, ignoring the shouts, ignoring the threats, ignoring the burning in my muscles as I tear up the road.

Until a man crashes into my legs and we tumble over. I try to scramble free but he has me tight. Another officer arrives and yanks my hands hard behind my back. I feel metal round my wrists then they haul me to my feet.

I roll on to my back and stare into the darkness. "We can't do it your way," I hiss. "It won't work."

Ronnie is nervous. He wants to run, but it is the wrong thing to do. "Trust me," I say. "The police will have you in less than fifteen seconds. Wait here," I insist. "They may go in a minute."

They won't go in a minute, but it is what I need to say to stop him running. I look again at the cars. There were two officers in the car on the left, another behind it and the last two standing between the cars. So there is more space to the right. I calm myself again and concentrate, waiting until my heart is still. I am locked in place.

I creep forward until I can hear voices and the buzz of radios. Somewhere, a phone goes off, but I ignore it and crawl to the edge of the light. And then I burst out, running as fast as I can, like the winds of hell are on my back. I make it to the cars before the police react, then swerve to the right. A woman officer turns, moving instinctively but then hesitating, because her view is blocked by the other cars. Then she yells and all the heads turn at once. I race round the right-hand car, leaning on the bonnet, then accelerating away. I hear the slam of a door from the other side, then shouts behind me and footsteps as they give chase. Then the burst of an engine.

I turn into the street Ronnie showed me, forcing my body faster as I see the church up ahead. I turn left as a car pulls alongside me, blue light spilling over the street as its tyres screech. I see the BMW parked ahead.

The police car slews across the road in front of me. I swerve but can't avoid it, rolling up over the bonnet then hitting the ground hard. The door opens and I see a dark uniform as it crashes down on top of me, rolling me over and yanking my hands hard behind my back. I feel metal round my wrists then they haul me to my feet.

I roll over again and stare out in front. Ronnie hisses at me. "You move too much," he says. "Keep still."

I glare at him and think about going on my own but I need this guy for now. "OK," I say. "Here's what we do. We creep forward on the right-hand side until I say, then we run, as fast as we can. I will be behind you but don't slow down."

He looks at me like I'm insulting him. "That is just as terrible as my plan," he says. "We do it—"

But I grab his shoulder to interrupt him. "WAIT!" I hiss. "Turn your phone off!"

Panic fills his eyes and he yanks his phone up and flicks it to silent just as it starts buzzing.

"How did you—?" he starts, but I ignore him.

"We do my plan," I say. "Let's go."